Jennifer Johnston is recognised as one of Ireland's finest writers. Her other books include *The Captains and the Kings*, *The Gates*, *How Many Miles to Babylon?*, *Shadows on our Skin* (which was shortlisted for the Booker Prize in 1977), *The Old Jest* (winner of the 1979 Whitbread Award for Fiction), *The Railway Station Man*, *Fool's Sanctuary*, *The Invisible Worm* (which was shortlisted for the *Sunday Express* Book of the Year in 1991) and *The Illusionist*, and, most recently, *Two Moons*.

The
Christmas
Tree

Jennifer Johnston

review

First published in Great Britain in 1981
by Hamish Hamilton

First published in this edition in 1999
by REVIEW

An imprint of Headline Book Publishing

10 9 8 7 6 5 4 3 2 1

ISBN 0 7472 6258 6

Typeset by Avon Dataset Ltd, Bidford-on-Avon, Warks

Printed and bound in Great Britain by
Clays Ltd, St Ives plc.

Headline Book Publishing
A division of Hodder Headline PLC
338 Euston Road
London NW1 3BH

www.reviewbooks.com
www.hodderheadline.co.uk

For P and U, S, L and M
with a lot of love

It was always a great day when the Christmas tree was brought into the house. The fresh smell of pine needles in the winter rooms; the excitement of unwrapping the sparkling glass ornaments from the tissue paper in which they had been so carefully packed eleven months before; the warm waxy smell as the tiny red corkscrew candles flicker for the first time in their scalloped holders. Those early days of the tree were almost better than Christmas itself, which never really came up to anyone's expectations. I must pull myself together and get a tree, something manageable, something I can cope with on my own, something that will cause no anxiety to Bibi. The latter, of course, may not be possible. I will use electric tree lights, not candles. I will assure her of that.

Yes, I think I must get a tree.

Re-creation.

All that is left.

*　*　*

I wrote last night to Jacob Weinberg. I have often wondered if that was his real name or not, but I see no reason why he should have lied to me. I was the one who was telling the lies. Maybe I have left it too late, but at least I don't think I will have too long to be worrying.

Perhaps my letter will follow him round the world for several months, but when he gets it, when it catches up with him I know that he will come. I have to know that. I do know that. The electric tree lights will glitter, and he will come. I sat up through the night, the whiskey very close to hand, propped into a sitting position with seven pillows. From time to time I dozed into a curious world of rushing, stumbling people, but never really slept with either conviction or peace. It was still dark when I finished the letter. I must have had quite a large amount of whiskey by then because I got out of bed and pulled a yellow blanket round me, put on my slippers and I went out of the house and down the steps along the icy path and out of the gate to the post-box that stands about ten yards up the road. It wasn't raining, but the air was very cold and I could hear the fog horns in the bay moaning in the distance, old ghosts. The letter fluttered down through the empty darkness and then there was silence and it was very cold, bitter silence. My hands under the sodium lights looked already dead. The moaning recommenced and I struggled back to bed.

A copy of the letter written to Jacob Weinberg on 18 December 1978.

'Dear Jacob,

I am sending this to your address in London in the hope that it may find you there. That is the address you gave me almost two years ago, telling me as you did so that though you seldom lived there for very long at a time, it was your home, your hole in case of panic, your gesture of Britishness. You never seemed to me to be a person who would suffer from panic; loneliness, nightmares, sorrow, but never panic. Of course, I didn't know you very well. I never allowed myself to know anyone very well. By now you will have looked hopelessly at the end of the letter to see who on earth it is from, like so many people turn to the last page of a detective story before they begin to read it, unable to bear the thought of two hundred and fifty pages of suspense. I presume, now you have seen my name, that you remember me. Not that there is very much to remember. Maybe you were angry with me when I left and that would add a sharpness to your memories, that indifference always fails to do.

I remember the umbrellas in the square and the small metal tables, the young brown boys diving into the harbour from the green and yellow and red painted boats and the smell of fish and drying nets. When you finally know for certain that you will never see a place again, images of it push their way into your mind, fighting for your attention. The very old cannot escape from images of their past, their youth, their full days. It is now the same with me. The thousand pieces of a jigsaw puzzle lie in front of me, scattered faces, voices, dreams, deaths, births, mistakes. Don't get me wrong, I'm not looking for sympathy, I merely want you, of all people, to understand. Merely is a nice word that people use at times like this, a word to take the heat out of whatever situation may be building up. I will come to the point. Too many rambling thoughts become a bore so quickly. I was never particularly honest with you. I never told you for instance that I had a plan . . . that you were to be the father of my child. I have never had courage of that sort. I have never had courage of any sort, that has been the absurdity of my life. Being a reasonably sensible man you would have undoubtedly refused to take part in my plan, so I lied. It would have changed the pattern of things if you had agreed and have involved us both in a situation that I think neither of us would really have enjoyed. And eventually you would have been mixed up in my rather messy end . . . which I must say quickly was not part of my plan.

You were sitting at the small round table with an empty coffee cup and a glass of wine beside you, writing something in that notebook you had always with you. You looked up and stared without seeing it at the small church across the harbour. At that moment, up above us, on the hill the cathedral bell tolled six o'clock . . . the angelus, it is called here, and people used to pause and bless themselves and then go on with life again. They don't do that any more . . . Then I knew you were the man I needed. How strange to think that, if the bell hadn't tolled at that moment, such a thought might never have entered my head. Instead of blessing myself, which has never been one of my preserving gestures, I crossed my fingers and hoped that you spoke English. I must say you didn't look as if it was very likely. So . . . we have a child, a daughter to be precise. She is now almost nine months old and already has your black, waving hair and your rabbinical nose. The only attribute she seems to have inherited from me is the size of her feet, large, well shaped. She will be able to walk for miles. Her hands, also, are large. They spread right across the palms of my hands and right from the day she was born had an amazing power in them. I haven't given her a name yet. Not personally, I mean. She is officially registered in London with the name of Anna Keating. I always intended to change her name when I got used to her being around, but when I found out about my condition I decided that you should call her what you wanted, probably after some stoical ancestress from some eastern European ghetto . . . something faintly exotic and very ethnic. She is yours. It makes me smile to think of her in years to come towering over you as you both walk together down some street. I do hope she will be intelligent as well as tall. She is yours. I repeat it as it has to sink in. She is yours. You must come at once and take her away. I am no longer able to care for her and she is temporarily at the home of my sister. Temporarily is the word she, my sister Bibi, uses as her major pretence is that I will soon be well again and then will be able to assume my unsatisfactory way of living. If only I could co-operate, I would be well in no time at all. My mother co-operated and they managed to prolong her pain and humiliation for six months. We smile and lie to each other and the child waits for you, becoming more and more aware of the world around her. I haven't seen her for some weeks now, so she will probably have forgotten about my inadequacies as a mother.

Bibi has behaved amazingly well about the whole situation for someone who doesn't like the rules to be broken. We have never been friends, but she is doing her duty now with a grace and kindness that make me feel guilty in my refusal to do what is expected of me. Her own children are in the process of growing up, so it is very generous of her to take my child and make her part of her family . . . welcome her. You don't really have to worry if you don't want to come and take the baby. She will be all right. Her future is assured. She will be brought up nicely. She will be taught to be truthful, charitable and responsible. To be a lady. She will go to the Convent of the Holy Child in Killiney, and no one will have the bad taste to mention her nose or her deep-set black foreign eyes. She will be secure. This is after all what every right-minded person wants for their children. The best. I never wanted it for myself, but maybe you will see things differently. It is up to you. To be mundane, what little money I possess goes to the child. It is not much, but it will keep whatever wolves there may be from the door.

I am very tired now. Looking back over this letter I see that I have failed to explain to you, except in a rather oblique way, that I am dying. We have all become so oblique about it that I find it rather hard to be blunt myself. You have no need to feel alarm for me. I am not afraid of death, it seems to me to be an attractive alternative to life, which I have never found very satisfactory. This process though, I find painful, messy and demoralising. Perhaps it will be quick.

The hand with which I hold the pen has become so heavy that I can barely drag it across the page. I will get up now and go to the post-box with this letter. I think that would be the safest thing to do.

It is not too far to go. It has been snowing and the east wind finds its pernicious way through every window. I will go back to bed then and wait for the daylight. They come and bring me fruit and little dishes they have made for me ... and flowers. I have a lot of flowers. I promise to eat their food to make them happy. I laugh to make them happy. I put their flowers in vases to make them happy. And then they go away and I am left alone.

I can see little fragments of the past. They bud and flower and fade in my mind, so I am never really alone.

I hope that you will come. I hope that you will forgive me.

Yours sincerely, Constance Keating.'

*   *   *

Constance's mother always had ladies in for bridge on Tuesday afternoons. Three tables of four placed around the drawing room, displacing the normal symmetry of the room. The tables were covered with green velvet cloths, with gold braided edges and gold tassels at each corner. One was placed in the bay window, overlooking the garden, one close to the fireplace, the most comfortable table in the winter, and the third was in the centre of the room, behind the sofa and under the Waterford glass chandelier.

At four-thirty exactly, Teresa would bring in a series of silver trays that held the tea, pale China, the cakes, the sandwiches and the hot, newly baked scones. The ladies would leave their tables and gather round the fire to fortify themselves for the next hour's mental exercise. Bibi and Constance were expected to come in at this moment and unobtrusively hand round the plates and the three-tiered cake stand. They were never allowed to pass the tea cups in case of accidents. They wore their tidy dresses and their patent leather shoes with straps across the instep. There was a short time when their mother used to insist on them being dressed alike, but neither girl took very kindly to this, so it was a phase that didn't last very long. Some of the older ladies would wear hats, neat, unflamboyant hats, with dark curling feathers growing from them or bunches of cloth flowers. Constance's mother never wore a hat, except to church on Sundays, or to weddings, or to the important functions that she attended from time to time with Father. Her hats were never sombre, and were, according to Father who paid the bills, incredibly expensive.

'And what have you been doing all afternoon, Constance?'

She had a greeny bronze feather curling over her left ear.

What a pretty bird it must have come from, Constance thought. Her fingers itched to touch it.

'It is Constance? Isn't it?'

Constance dragged her eyes from the feather and looked down at her feet. One white sock was edging its way down towards her ankle.

'Constance!' said Mother sharply.

'We went to the park,' Constance whispered.

'How lovely,' said the lady, with amazing enthusiasm. 'A lovely thing to do.'

'She's shy,' said Bibi, with contempt. She was dutifully passing the hot buttered scones from lady to lady. Tiny white handkerchiefs wiped the butter from finger tips.

'And what did you do in the park?'

Constance scowled at her feet.

'We fed the ducks.' Bibi spoke for her.

Some of the drakes had been green and bronze, Constance remembered. She raised her eyes towards the hat again.

'Then,' said Bibi, who liked the sound of her own voice, 'we played grandmother's footsteps on the steps near the pond and Constance fell and hurt her knee.'

'Oh, poor Constance.'

Constance wondered if she had killed the duck herself . . .

'It bled all over her socks.'

. . . with her own bare hands.

'I hope it's feeling better now, Constance.'

Creeping up behind the unsuspecting creature, like grandmother's footsteps.

'She's lost her tongue.'

Then . . .

'Constance, if you can't be polite, you must leave the room.'

. . . pounce.

'She's sweet. Such lovely fair hair.'

The lady stretched out a hand to stroke the hair and Constance burst into a storm of tears.

'Go to Nanny. Silly, silly child. Go.' Mother's voice was exasperated.

*   *   *

The doctor walked in through the hall door. I heard his footsteps coming towards me across the hall. He pushed open my bedroom door and came over to the bed. He stood in silence looking down at me until I opened my eyes and looked up at him. We have known each other too long for there to be any formality in our relationship.

'Do they still have ducks in Herbert Park?'

He nodded. He didn't really look very surprised. I think he stopped being surprised by me a long time ago.

He sat down on the bed beside me and took hold of my wrist.

His eyes had that preoccupied look that doctors' eyes get at such moments.

'I suppose the children feed them, just like they used to?'

'Much more likely to throw stones at them, if you ask me.'

He'd always been a mildly gloomy sort of fellow.

'Monday and Wednesdays,' I remembered. His fingers were cold on my wrist. 'And then Tuesdays and Fridays we went to Sandymount and walked along the edge of the sea. If the weather was good we were allowed to take our shoes off and play on the sand. We didn't go there in the real summer though, there were always such huge crowds on the strand. We might have caught something dreadful. Nits or something.'

'A possibility I suppose.'

'Brown paper bags full of bread. Do you remember that awful grey wartime bread? Only fit for the ducks, Nanny used to say. We had to fold the bags up carefully and bring them home again. That was the war too. No paper . . . something like that. Do you remember . . . ?'

'You're behaving like an old woman. Stop it.' His voice was sharp.

'Isn't it strange? I find myself very pre-occupied with the past. I suppose when you've no future ahead it's natural to run to the past. Try to make a little sense out of it . . . even just re-play it . . . like home movies.'

'All this nonsense about no future. Death.'

He dropped my hand on the bed and rubbed fretfully at the side of his nose with his forefinger.

'Oh, Bill . . . surely you don't subscribe to Bibi's fantasy that I have a long and merry life ahead of me?'

'One must never give up hope.'

He spoke without conviction. His eyes were the colour of sea-washed pebbles. So long ago they had been a bright, almost alarming blue.

'My one hope is to die as soon as possible. My noble aspiration. Let's have a drink? I could do with a drink.'

He nodded.

I struggled up from the bed. I had a terrible feeling for a moment, as my feet connected with the ground, that I was going to do something undignified, like throw up all over him, but the feeling passed after a moment or two. He watched every movement that I made, like a very young man watches his newest love.

'Come into the other room. This is so bloody squalid.'

In what had once been my father's study, the evening sun was fading through the windows. The books, the shelves and the ornate marble mantelpiece were covered with a layer of dust. I must get down to it, I thought. If I were to meet my father in the near future I wouldn't like to have it on my conscience that I had left his room in such a dreary state. The fruit trees need to be pruned too. I must make a list. The bare branches had that whippy unproductive look about them. Bill coughed or something and I remembered him. I sat down in a chair by the window. Had my father not died he would have been sitting in it now, a book in his hand, a glass of very dry sherry on the small table beside him. He would have been very displeased with me ... or maybe not ... maybe the secret person behind the dry, elegant façade would not have been displeased. The bare black branches stretched towards the sky. Snow clouds were building up. Soon the setting sun would be demolished.

'What's up?'

I jumped.

'I'm sorry.'

'You're distraite this evening. Are you feeling very bad?'

'No. No. Just a wandering mind. That's all. You pour the drinks. I've always been hopeless at pouring drinks. There should be water in the jug. I'll have mine straight. Is it cold in here?'

He looked at the half empty bottle on the table and then picked it up and unscrewed the lid.

'I hope you're not hitting it too hard.'

I smiled and didn't answer; after all, what was the point? After a moment he smiled too, for the first time since he had come in to the house.

'No, it's not cold.'

'I could do something with the fire if you liked.'

He shook his head and handed me my drink.

'It's boiling in here.'

I giggled.

'Bibi'll kill me when she sees the electricity bill.'

He pulled over a chair and sat down beside me.

'What used you to do on Thursday afternoons?'

'Thursday . . . ? Oh, yes. It was Nanny's day off. We used to play in the garden and have tea in the kitchen. I wrote to the child's father today.'

There was a long silence. The first trickle of whiskey down my throat made me feel good.

'Yes,' he said. 'Yes. What did you say?'

'I told him . . . He didn't know, you see . . . I hadn't . . .'

He frowned slightly.

'I told him . . . well . . . the situation as I see it. I asked him to come and collect her.'

'What on earth do you think Barbara will have to say about that?' He had never called her Bibi, but then, of course, neither had my father.

'I suppose she'll go crazy to begin with, but in the end . . . after all it can't be much fun being lumbered with someone else's child for life. In the end . . .'

'You have a tendency to ride rough-shod over people, Constance. It's always been . . . well . . .'

'One of my many faults.'

'I wouldn't say that, quite. But . . . I can't help thinking of the man . . . the father, suddenly faced with . . . you must admit it will be a terrible shock. A terrible shock. I mean to say . . .'

He took a rapid gulp of whiskey.

'He can always tear the letter up and forget about the whole thing.'

'Don't be silly. That's such a silly thing to say.'

'I didn't mean it to happen like this. You know that. I didn't know what was going to . . . strike me. I had the future all planned.'

'If I may ask a personal question . . . how long . . . how long?' His face reddened as he spoke. The unbearable reticence of the Irish invaded his whole body. He picked up his glass and took another gulp and choked.

'Just long enough to get pregnant. I was lucky. It takes some people ages. Months. I was lucky.'

He stopped coughing and laughed.

'You're a terror.'

'Let's have another drink.'

He took my glass and filled it, and his own.

'That's your lot then.'

'I shouldn't think so. When you've gone I will carry the bottle in to the other room and put it beside my bed. I might even bring another bottle in if I don't consider there's enough left in that one. Enough to be of any use. Your pills don't always work very well you know. The nights are long. Dark.'

He frowned into his glass.

'Too long,' I said, wanting some reaction from him.

'Come off it, Constance,' was all he said.

I leant past him and fumbled with the light switch. My hand felt heavy and unmanoeuvreable. The bones and ligaments were barely held together now by sick, stretched skin. After what seemed like a long time, the light came on.

'I must get a Christmas tree.'

He shook his head.

'I've arranged for you to go into hospital the day after tomorrow.'

'Nothing huge. Just a small one to put on that table in the window. Christmas isn't Christmas . . .'

'Constance.'

'A real tree. Some people buy plastic ones. I want a real tree.'

'Constance.'

He looked unhappy. I touched his knee with a finger.

'No, Bill. I'll be all right here, you know.'

'You're not all right. You can't look after yourself any more. You know that as well as I do. More and more you need care, nursing. Don't be tiresome about this, Constance, please. You should be in hospital. I should have been firm when you came back first. You should have gone straight in then. But you . . . you . . .'

'I bullied you.'

'It would be so much easier . . .'

'Don't bother appealing to my better nature. I have none. I'll clean this place up, if that's what's bothering you. I won't bother you with calls in the middle of the night. Just get me a Christmas tree, that's all I want you to do.'

'You need to be cared for.'

'I care for nobody, no not I, and nobody cares for me. Do you remember, Bill, that you asked me to marry you?'

'It's the sort of thing one tends to remember.'

'God, that was a long time ago. How lucky you were that I said no. Were you broken-hearted?'

'I don't think so. I can't really remember that.'

'You should have been broken-hearted.'

'I was never as flamboyant as you.'

'Was I? What a lovely thought. I always looked upon myself as a very ordinary person. Was that why you wanted to marry me? My flamboyance?'

'I don't know any longer. Attraction of opposites perhaps . . . Only you weren't attracted to me.'

'Oh, I was. I really was. I just didn't want to get married, be . . .'

He smiled.

'Good days.'

'Angela was a better wife for you, I think. You had some hope with her of being happy ever after. Are you happy ever after?'

'I . . .'

'Don't tell me if you're not. Tonight I don't want to know things like that.'

'I am. I am. Rich, successful, esteemed. What more can anyone want?'

'What indeed?'

'The day after tomorrow.'

'No, Bill. My answer remains the same. It's my life, my . . . well you know . . . the word no one will allow me to use. I prefer my pig-sty to your hospital. I have my faculties intact. I can choose.'

'Be realistic . . . and don't change the subject this time. The time may come . . . has to come when you can't do anything for yourself. When you have to have help. When you can't do the basic . . . For heaven's sake, Constance, you know what I mean. Don't make me spell it out.'

'Get me a nurse then. A nun. A housekeeper. All of them if necessary. I'm not going into hospital. I don't want to die in hospital. I don't want professional sympathy, sterile hands, needles, tubes and bed pans.'

'It would be so much easier . . .'

'I know. The facts of death are very disagreeable. I am very tired now. Finish your drink and go home, please.' He just fidgeted with his glass uneasily. He was going to get big stick from Bibi.

'Get me a girl, if it makes you happier. Not someone all starched if possible, just a girl to be here. A nice girl. Perhaps someone who can write . . . read and write. I suppose most people can do that nowadays. It might come in handy. I don't want to be constantly disinfected.'

He took my hand for a few seconds and held it.

'You always were heap big trouble.'

We both laughed in a half-hearted way.

'Perhaps I was broken-hearted.'

I shook my head.

'Not for more than about a week, if that.'

'I insist. I remember the pain.'

'Absolute rot. It was a bruise, rather than a break.'

'Let me help you to bed.'

'No, I can manage. I like to do things at my own speed. I may sit here all night. After all, going to bed at night and getting up in the morning is only a social habit, like eating three meals a day and brushing your teeth.'

'What am I to say to Barbara?'

'That's your problem.'

'And Angela . . .'

'Go home, Bill.'

He emptied his glass and stood up.

'You really . . .'

'Next time you come, bring me a Christmas tree.'

*   *   *

Snow drifted slowly down through the bare branches of the trees. It floated into the light from the street lamps and landed and lay thinly on the statues, the few parked cars and filled the resting tramlines. The wide street was empty and very quiet. For once there were no drunks, tramps, tinkers or cabbies hunched about their half-starved horses to be seen. They had sensibly moved to whatever form of shelter was available to them, homes or doss-houses or holes in a wall somewhere. On the bridge, a tall cowboy in a ten-gallon hat and a small red Indian woman, boot-polish brown and feathers in her hair, were wrapped together in a large plaid rug. They leant on the balustrade of the bridge and stared sleepily down into the water. Flakes of snow hovered and then landed on the river's brown surface and then disappeared, absorbed, moved slowly towards the sea. The great clouds above were stained with the reflected light of the sleeping city.

'It's never proper snow,' complained the woman. 'Hardly ever. Thick crunchy snow like the icing sugar on a Christmas cake. It's hardly ever like that. We are deprived. It's most unfair.'

'I say, thank God.'

'We just get 'flu and chilblains and horrid east winds and red noses and filthy brown slush.'

The cowboy dropped a cigarette butt into the river. It flashed for a moment as it fell, and then like the snowdrops disappeared.

'Me like heap snow. Me like heap big sleighs pulled by horses with jingling bells.'

'Christmas card stuff. Bumble, bumble.'

'How unromantic you are. Heap lot unromantic.'

There was a long silence. Up the river a bell rang half past something.

'The damp is starting to creep through the rug. My shoulders are getting damp. Heap damp.'

'Constance.'

There was an even longer silence. She moved uneasily under the rug, disengaging herself from contact with his warm body.

'What?'

'Would you marry me? I mean . . . would you . . . well . . . ?'

'No.'

'No?' His voice was slightly surprised. 'Just like that?'

'There's not much one can say . . . I mean . . . it's either yes or no, isn't it?'

'You haven't even thought about it. Think about it. Say that you'll think about it, please.'

'I don't have to think about it. No.'

Another pause.

'But thank you just the same. Thank you, Bill.'

'What does thank you mean?'

'Oh hell, Bill, it means I can't think of anything else to say. It means thank you anyway for . . .'

'It . . . we could . . . Constance . . . why not?'

'Lots of reasons. I don't want to marry anyone. Anyone. It's not just you. I don't love you. No. Truly.'

'I thought you loved me. I thought . . . we . . . you've . . . I love you very much.'

'I love you. I like you. But not the sort of love you mean. I'm sorry.'

She took his hand and squeezed it under the rug.

'Oh God,' she said, 'I hate this.'

She laughed abruptly.

'What a horrible thing to say. It just slipped out. Being a cause of misery doesn't appeal to me at all. I feel sick. Believe me Bill, dear Bill. I'd cause you real misery if I said yes. This at least will only be temporary.'

'Temporary.' He spoke the word with contempt.

'Me heap big trouble.'

The snow was transforming itself into needles of sleet. Not romantic in any way.

'Why do you say things like that about yourself? I know you. I know we could be happy.'

'Nobody knows that. Nobody knows anything . . . until perhaps it's too late. Me heap cold. Please take me home. Take heap big trouble home.'

He seemed hypnotised by the flowing water. For a moment the crazy thought entered her head that he might be contemplating suicide. She nudged him with her elbow.

'Bill.'

'I don't think you take me seriously,' he said gloomily.

'I do. I promise I do. And me, I take me seriously. You're behaving a bit badly. Why don't you take me seriously and believe me when I say no?'

'Because I don't think you know your own mind.'

'I'm learning about it. Feeling my way. The answer is no.' She pulled the rug from his shoulders and wrapped it round herself.

'No,' she said as she walked away across the bridge. 'No. No. No.' She didn't look back, because she knew that in his ten-gallon hat and his leather waistcoat, six-guns neatly balancing each other on his hips, he looked ludicrous, vulnerable and there was the terrible possibility that she might go back to him, through the brown slush and the sleet and put her arms around him and say, yes, safety, oh yes. Yes.

*   *   *

I must have slept a little because I jumped out of a sort of fuddled comfort when the telephone rang. I was stiff all over. It seemed to take me about five minutes to get across the room. Any normal person would have rung off.

'What is all this?'

I could hear Bibi's angry voice before I got the receiver half way to my ear.

'What's the time?'

'Eleven. Five past eleven.'

She was always very precise. I still had all night ahead of me.

'I've been talking to Bill. He says . . .'

'I'm really being very difficult.'

'Something along those lines. I'm glad you are aware . . . Honestly, Constance, you behave as if we were all plotting against you. As if . . .'

'You are really, aren't you?'

'We are only trying to do what is best for you. We're thinking of you. If you would only let us help you.'

'If you would only leave me alone.'

'A couple of weeks in hospital and you'll be as right as rain. You're not giving yourself a chance.'

I didn't say anything.

'The private wing in Vincents is lovely. Everyone says so. I've visited lots of people there. It's not like being in hospital at all really . . . You would have privacy . . . privacy . . . they would look after you. I know you value privacy . . . Constance, you're not listening, I know you're not listening.'

'How's the child?'

'Very good indeed. She's settled in well. The children love her. Even Charles is getting very attached to her. She's as good as gold. You needn't worry about her at all.'

'I don't. I just . . .'

'She's going to be terribly spoiled, everyone makes such a fuss of her. There's one thing . . .'

There was a delicate pause.

'Yes? What's that?'

'Well . . . shouldn't she be christened, Constance? I mean to say . . . We should make some arrangements . . .'

'That can wait.'

'One wouldn't want to leave it too long, dear.'

'For heaven's sake, Bibi, leave that. Time enough for christenings later on.'

'But . . .'

'Time enough for salvation later on. Bill is going to bring me a Christmas tree. Isn't that nice of him?'

'You're always so unreasonable.'

'I don't think so.'

'Just the same as ever. If only for once, at this . . . if you'd try and see things from somebody else's point of view.'

'I'm sorry. Honestly Bibi . . .'

'Words, words, words. And now Bill says you want a housekeeper.'

'Not exactly that. A girl . . . a nice girl. Just for a short time.'

'I'll speak to Sister Aloysius in the morning. Maybe she can produce someone. As you say . . . a nice girl. Just till you're . . . better . . . able to manage.'

'You're very good. I really appreciate how good you are. Do you realise that?'

'After all, you are my sister.'

She sounded a little less angry.

'Even so. You could have washed your hands of me ages ago. Let me stew in my own juice. No one would have blamed you.' There was a long silence.

'I'll see you tomorrow,' said Bibi. 'I'll be over in the afternoon. Maybe . . .'

'I won't have changed my mind.'

I heard her sigh and then she put the receiver down. I sat for a short while by the phone. In my head something thudded. Give up, give up. Don't for heaven's sake keep on boring them like this.

They want to keep their spirits up. Don't you see. See. Shining aprons, teeth. Smiling. Everything's going to be all right. Needles. Needless needles carrying relief for them as well as you. Me. Shining sheets and lights and hands.

'I want to die in the dark.'

I woke myself as I spoke and then got up and went back to my chair by the window. Father's chair. The seat was still warm. I emptied the whiskey bottle into my glass and sat, staring out at the frosty stars. The seats in the Piazza del Porto had been warm and the wine in the bottle had been warm and the sun had turned the tourists' arms from cream to pink to brown and dried the red nets draped on the harbour wall. A cracked bell chimed up on the hill, and a small man called Jacob Weinberg frowned slightly as he wrote something in his notebook. Stars tremble as you watch them, or is it planets? I don't remember. I think it must be stars. Twinkle . . . twinkle . . . they're all at it. And the street-lights. They twinkle nicely. Between me and the twinkling world, something moved. It was my mother. She passed across in front of the window, her hair coiled like a sleeping snake at the back of her neck. She wore a long black crêpe dress that sighed as she moved. She didn't look in my direction.

'You shouldn't sit in your father's room, you know.'

She stared around, her face displeased.

'He hates people to use his room. Hates it to be disturbed.' She moved quickly to the fireplace and pulled the bell. I smiled.

'It will have to be cleaned up before he comes home.' She looked at me now, her eyes cool, no twinkling there.

'We don't want him to be upset.'

'Where is he?' I asked out of some sort of alcoholic devilment.

'Goodness gracious, I don't know where he is. Fishing or something. Staying with some lord or other. How would I know? It doesn't really matter, does it? I don't think you should use his room though. Why does no one come?' She moved towards the bell again.

'No one is in, Mother. It's all right. I'll tidy it all up before he comes.'

'No one? How very curious. There should be someone here.' She came a little closer to me and peered at my face in silence for a while. She looked puzzled.

'You've let yourself go. You always needed to take care of yourself.' She thought for a moment. 'How old are you now?'

'Forty-five.'

'My goodness. Forty-five. You really must pull yourself together. When I was your age . . .' Her face blurred, slipped out of focus for a moment. She held out a pale glimmering hand towards me.

'It . . . is . . . Constance? Constance . . .'

Her eyes became like stars, or was it perhaps planets. A cloud obscured the moon. Her dress melted into darkness, and the coiled snake of her hair and the hand held out to me, all became night and her eyes last of all dimmed leaving silence and emptiness in the dark room. The cloud moved on and shadows of the bare branches made a pattern on the floor. I could hear the clock in St Bartholomew's chime . . . three, four.

If only it were possible to choose your time to die, I thought, this would be a good moment. A time to be born and a time to die. Only you hadn't the right to choose. All the other choices that you had fought to be allowed to make, were all irrelevant in the end. Someone else made this choice. The last door was the one you couldn't open for yourself. The thin sharp edge of a knife was drawn through my gut. As the first shock of the pain subsided, I got my glass to my lips and finished the whiskey. Billy's useless pills were beside the bed. A time to kill and a time to heal. I didn't need to turn on the light. I knew my way even through the blackness of the hall. For a thousand years I had known my way through the blackness. A time to weep and a time to laugh; a time to mourn and a time to dance. I was too tired by the time I reached my bed to take off my jumper, but I unpinned my trousers and got in between the sheets. Last week's sheets. Who cares? I shook three of the pills out into my hand and washed them down my throat with a glass of water.

* * *

'There is no need to look so gloomy,' said Mother. 'Absolutely no need.'

Constance didn't answer. She stared across the drawing room at an unfamiliar figure. Hair prinked, yellow taffeta dress, lipstick. Just a touch of lipstick. Perhaps that was what was wrong. The lipstick. She gnawed at it with her bottom teeth. Mother sighed.

'You look as if you were going to be executed, for heaven's sake.'

'I don't think yellow suits me.'

'Nothing'll suit you if you insist on looking so disagreeable. Smile. You're going to a party. Smile . . . or something.'

The yellow figures smiled at each other. It didn't seem to make any difference.

'That's better.'

A lie, thought Constance. A damn lie. Things hadn't seemed quite so bad up in her bedroom. There hadn't been so much light for one thing.

'Keep smiling. It makes no end of a difference.'

The door opened and Bibi came in. Her dress wasn't yellow. It looked marvellous. She also had the advantage of having done the whole thing many times before.

'Have a glass of sherry, dear, and tell Constance not to be silly. She's being fearfully silly. She says she doesn't want to go.'

'I never wanted to go. You blooming well insisted that I had to. I can't stand Patricia O'Mahony. I won't know anyone there. I hate all that slow quick quick slow stuff and this is a horrible dress. Horrible.'

'You're being tiresome and boring, Constance. You'll enjoy yourself when you get there. You know that. It's a sweet dress. Isn't it sweet, Bibi?'

'It's a pity it's yellow,' said Bibi unhelpfully, as she poured herself a glass of sherry.

'Don't be unkind, dear.' Mother's face had a glimmer of a smile as she spoke. 'It's lovely. Just relax. Don't brood, dear, or sulk . . . you're getting too old for sulking now. Just keep smiling.'

'It honestly didn't look too bad in the shop. The best of . . .'

'If you like,' suggested Bibi, with sudden and unexpected kindness, 'I'll let you borrow my blue crêpe. I know you like it. It's more your colour.'

'Don't encourage her, Bibi. She's perfectly all right as she is. She just has to learn to pull herself together. To be shy is one thing, Constance . . . I was very shy when I was your age . . .' Another damn lie thought Constance bitterly.

'But I made every effort . . . You are deliberately difficult. Obtuse you might say.'

Constance turned away from the glass. Blue crêpe, yellow sackcloth . . . it didn't make much difference.

'I bet Ingrid Bergman never looked like this,' she said. Bibi laughed. Mother tutted and went and poured herself another gin and tonic.

'The great thing is . . .' There was a hissing sound as she opened the tonic bottle '. . . to feel you look marvellous and then everybody thinks you do. I look marvellous. I am marvellous. It sort of flows out of you towards the whole world and they . . . become . . . well, engulfed in it. It's a sort of confidence trick really. I am marvellous.'

She meant every word of it. She put the bottle back on the silver tray and took a sip of her drink.

'I am marvellous,' sang Bibi, and did a slow, quick, quick, slow across the room. She was wearing a pair of Mother's pre-war black satin evening sandals with little diamante buckles on them that sparkled as her feet moved. The door opened and Father put his head round it.

'Are the girls ready? I told Henry Barrington I'd be at the club by eight-thirty.'

'Coats. They just need their coats.'

He came into the room and looked at his daughters.

'Goodness gracious, how grown up you both look. It makes me feel very old. Old.'

He smoothed at his hair with a hand.

'I've never seen you in yellow before, Constance.'

'Get your coats, girls, your father is in a hurry. It suits her doesn't it? I was just telling her how much it suits her. Coats, dears.'

'Old.'

His hair was greying in the most distinguished manner behind his ears. That was the only sign of age.

'I don't . . .' began Constance.

'Don't keep your father waiting, dear. Run along and get your coat.'

'I won't be back before about midnight. Don't wait up for me.'

'No. I certainly wouldn't do that.'

*　*　*

I'm going to take boom boom a sentimental journey boom
　　Gonna put my heart at ease
　　Going to take boom boom . . .
　　Straight from the bath, eyes, ears, fingernails shinily scrubbed
　　A sentimental journey boom.
　　To renew . . .
Young men from the safety of their numbers, glasses clamped between damp, nervous fingers, talked about rugby or red MG sports-cars or nothing, eyeing all the time the butterfly girls.

Old mehemories Boomy da boom. Crash.

Massed flowers in the corners of the room trembled to the music. Six young men in maroon jackets plucked and struck and puffed and the sound hurled its way through the crowded room and down the stairs and out into the street, calling to the stragglers, the feet draggers. Such fun. Such such boomy fun. Girls massed by the azaleas trembled also in fear that they would . . . oh God, please God, I'll do anything, anything . . . be left, yellow or blue or green, alone by the flowers. Waiters carried red wine, white wine on silver trays, tumblers of cup, filled with cherries, oranges, apples, mint leaves, lemon slices, each one a meal in itself.

Boom boom a sentimental journey

Will you . . . ?

Oh thank you, God.

Gonna put my boomy boomy

One and two and . . . sorry

Is it better than total rejection? Is it. Ooops. Just, only just. Less humiliating.

Do you hunt?

No.

Expand, Mother would say. Smile. Tell the boring creep why you don't hunt. Tell him you hate horses. Make a joke. Tell him you can't stand killing things. Smile. Tell him the thought of chasing a fox round then watching him being torn to bits by a pack of hounds makes you sick.

Boomy crash.

I say . . . sorry. I hope I . . . splendid band.

Ask him if he believes in capital punishment. Smile. Tell him . . .

To renew old mehemories bang bang bang crash.

Thanks awfully.

Back to the azaleas.

Old, old young men, hardened by a year or so on the battlefields of Europe, squashed their cigarettes out in the flower tubs and laced the cup with whiskey from the hip flasks hidden in their inside pockets, their eyes roving over the talent, their hopes fairly high.

Oh sleepy lagoon tarara the moon

Frightful band . . . what!

And two on an island

Bibi's diamante buckles glittered everywhere

Dadadadeeda

Oh sleepy lagoon

You Barbara Keating's sister?

Yes.

Oh.

Super girl, Barbara.

Well, what could you say to that?

And two on an island.

You in Trinity?

No.

Oh.

Oh sleeeeeepy lagoon

Jolly good band.

Bow ties slowly wilting like the flowers, or creeping sideways leaving Adams apples climbing desperately out of tight white collars.

Old, young men, not long out of khaki, cantered on the floor, hot cheeks pressed against the hot cheeks of girls who had never even thought of death. Hot fingers tentatively explored bare shoulders. Young, young men tried very hard to watch where they were putting their feet.

Scrumptious food, don't you think?

When will it all be over?

Are you going to the Bradleys on Tuesday?

No.

Smile.

You a sister of . . . ?

There's nothing left for me of all that used to be . . .

Did you have a brother in the Skins?

No.

Oh.

There's just a memory among . . .

Sorry.

My souvenirs.

Thanks awfully.

I hate azaleas. I will hate azaleas all my life.

Take your partners for The Walls of . . .

Hurray. Push up there a bit can't you. Here. Hands, hands.

Limerick.

Daaaaaa.

Walls spinning. Flowers spinning. Dizzy. Dawn spreading across the sky. Brave stars still sparkle like diamante shoe buckles.

Goodnight ladies, it's time to say goodnight.

See you next week at the Bradleys.

See you . . . see you . . . see . . .

Don't tell Mummy I danced all night with Charles Barry.

Sleepy, sparkling eyes.

Staircase creaking under tired feet.

Who's Charles Barry?

Sssssh.

Opal sky outside the landing window, stroked by orange rising fingers of the sun.

Why not anyway? What's wrong with . . . ?

Ssssssssh.

Bibi?

You'll wake them. He's divine. Divine. The most . . . oh ssssh.
But . . .
He digs with the other foot.
Goodnight ladies. It's time to say goodnight.

* * *

I awoke to hear the milkman whistling as he and his bottles rattled
up the path of the house next door. He didn't come to me any more,
milk makes me feel sick . . . not just feel sick, throw up viciously. I
felt empty, painless and almost light-hearted. I got up and pinned
myself into my trousers once more. I would follow my ghostly
mother's instructions and clean my father's room. Maybe he was
planning to make me a visit as she had done, I doubted it though. I
collected together the paraphernalia of domesticity, buckets and
cloths, the hoover, fading yellow dusters, soap powder and polish. I
prepared to, to quote a much loved phrase of my old headmistress,
buckle down. Outside, snow flakes twisted unwillingly from a grim
sky. I'm dreaming of a white Christmas. Ding dong, ding dong.

In all those years there was only one I could remember. It must
have been during the war sometime. Father had come home on leave.
We had met him at the boat. I remember being disappointed when
he came down the gangway with his uniform in a brown paper parcel
under his arm, looking just the same as he had the day he went away.
It had been snowing then and the taxi's wipers had had great trouble
pushing the flakes backwards and forwards across the windscreen
and had groaned with the effort. My father looked brown and
complained about the cold.

I polished the small circular table on which my father used to
keep his legal papers and magazines. I dragged it over to the window.
I would put the Christmas tree on it. It would look good there and
the passers-by would be able to see the lights. Among the

photographs on the mantelpiece was one of my parents standing on the steps of the church after their wedding. Flowers, heavy lace and pointed white satin shoes. The sun must have been shining as my mother's eyes were slightly closed in protection against the dazzle. They both smiled straight into the camera, showing their teeth. A crowd of ladies and gentlemen, also smiling, hovered discreetly behind them. This is a happy day, everybody's faces said. I wiped the dust off with one of the yellow dusters and wondered why he had done it.

He should have remained a charming bachelor. He had no need for the cushioning against loneliness that marriage is supposed to bring; in fact, he greatly preferred his own company to being with her and he was constantly having to protect himself against the demands that his family made on him. He and my mother rarely had what people might call rows, but that was merely because they seldom spoke. They led their separate lives, they had their separate friends. They met at their own dinner parties and at those of others. There was no friction between them, only an unbridgeable distance; neither love nor hate, only a cool, well-mannered indifference. I used to dread the thought that at some stage I might myself become enmeshed in a similar relationship. The thing I didn't realise until much later was that they were not unhappy, neither of them in the end of all had wanted anything other than comfort and order.

I would get dressed, properly dressed. I had been wearing the same shirt and jumper for over a week now, never even taking them off when I fell into bed. I would have a huge hot bath and then dress myself in clean clothes and then when Bibi came I would ask her to take me into town. After all, what was the point of having a Christmas tree if you didn't have presents to put underneath it. Grafton Street would be lovely, lights and carol singers and the shops full of gay, extravagant nonsense. What could you buy a child of nine months? A

Teddy bear? Maybe she wouldn't be a Teddy bear sort of person. I hadn't been. The only thing I remember about my Teddy bear is the trouble I got into when I opened it up with scissors to find out what made the moaning noise when you tipped him backwards. Not a Teddy bear. Anyway, think of how Jacob would curse me when he had to struggle with a Teddy bear on the road to Mandalay or wherever he might find himself going.

The hoover made a terrible noise, roaring and crackling as it sucked up the debris of a month's neglect. I opened the window and a few tired snowflakes floated to the floor and then melted. The wind was bitter. The curtains moved, in spite of their weight, and my papers on the table by the fire rustled dangerously. I put a book on them to keep them under control and went across the hall to the kitchen. It would take days to get the smell of illness out of the house . . . and what was the point anyway? For how long would I feel light? A remission they called it, and with it, it seems, comes a great feeling of hope. A misleading feeling? Of course misleading. Days, weeks, possibly even months it might last, and you could make what you would of it. A lull or pause. My mother's remission had come too late. She had spent six months in pain and bewilderment, not understanding why she couldn't die. No pain. That to me would be a miracle. No fear of pain. To be able to forget the existence of pain. The only remission. To give knowledge of salvation unto His people by the remission of their sins through the tender mercy of our God . . . it went on, most beautiful and rhythmic words. How strange after so long that those words should come into my head. Whereby the dayspring from on high hath visited us, something, something, about the shadow of death. I went back into the study and took down the dictionary from the shelf. Heavy OED. I had to sit before I could open it and peer at the words. Forgiveness or pardon of sins or other offences. A decrease or subsidence in the violence of a disease or pain. The word temporary written in brackets. Maybe in my remission God would be remissful towards me. Maybe I will feel lighter yet. Maybe I'm potty.

I decided to scrub the kitchen floor. It was still only eight o'clock in the morning and no one would come near me for hours yet. Tender mercy was good, but when you looked around, inappropriate. Even God didn't seem to use too much of it. His demands seemed to me to be punishing. Unending. Bibi wouldn't agree, she would say you just need faith and leave it at that, but then she and I never had any point of agreement. 'Au contraire,' she used to say. 'Au contraire, darling.' Back in her Trinity days and her beautiful eyes would dazzle. It was an affectation she had for about a year. It was somehow more elegant than bluntly disagreeing and she had always disagreed with everyone except Charles Barry.

The horrible thing about scrubbing floors is that your hands get all wrinkled and stiff with the hot water and dirt, and the floor never seems to look much better when you've finished. I must buy some rubber gloves if I'm going to make a habit of buckling down.

I struggled with the kitchen window and it finally opened, letting in the sound of morning traffic with the wind. I finished the three rooms. I wondered if my mother would come and commend my industry. But it had never been her way, and I don't suppose her personality has changed much with several years of death.

The water came out of the bath tap in a brown flood, which gradually turned to city water colour. The room filled with comforting steam. I covered the long glass with a towel before taking off my clothes. The one thing I can't bear is my own emaciated appearance. It is no longer romantic and waif-like, just grotesque, a Hogarth victim. I wanted to remain unperturbed in my remission. It is not the thought of death that worries me, it is the process of dying.

*   *   *

'I don't understand.' Mother's voice was fretful.

The sweet smell of cut grass drifted on the warm air.

'Simply, simply don't understand. I thought you were enjoying Trinity.'

'I'm not getting anything out of it. I'm not putting anything into it either. I'm just so bored . . . I suppose that's the easiest word to use, with the whole process. I feel I'm wasting time. Time. I get the awful feeling sometimes that you might get punished for wasting too much time.'

'Don't be foolish, dear. Talking in riddles never got anyone anywhere.'

'I want to go away.'

'Away? Whatever for?'

'Too look.'

'Ttttt.'

'Can I stand on my own feet? Can I bear to live alone? Can I blooming grow up? Become a person?'

'Well, if you ask my opinion, you'll do all those things a lot better if you stick in College till you get your degree. You're immature. Far, far more immature than Bibi.'

'I'm not going back next term. If I have to look at those decrepit old men in their dirty gowns droning on about Shakespeare once more, I'll go potty. Drone, drone. We just sit there, hundreds of us writing down their boring words or sleeping, and they drone on, like bees in the distance. They don't even care whether we're interested or not. Oh God.'

'They are intelligent men. You have to learn . . .'

'I'm not going back, Mother.'

'Ttttt.'

At the far end of the garden Father and Bibi were loosening the tennis net and looping it up. Constance never really knew why you had to do that. Like so many things, it had to be done, no explanation was ever given.

'It's not as if you hadn't been passing your exams.'

Bibi laughed at something Father had said. The sound drifted with the smell of grass across the flower beds, an orderly sound.

'And you're having fun, aren't you? You always seem to be having fun. Dances and all that.'

'It's not a question of having fun.'

Father and Bibi were walking towards them. Bibi bounced a ball in front of her with her racquet, as a child might have done.

'If you wait and do your degree, you'll be qualified.'

'Qualified for what?'

'Constance, you can be so exasperating. I don't know where you get it from. Bibi has a good job. Bibi's friends have good jobs or they're married. It's only sensible to be qualified.'

'I don't want to be someone's superior secretary.'

'There's . . .'

'Or a teacher. Or a social worker.'

'What do you want to do?'

'I've told you . . . go away. Look.'

Bibi and Father arrived and sat down beside them in the waiting deck-chairs. They were pink, but not hot.

'Who won?' asked Constance.

'He walloped me.'

'I beat her nicely.' He looked pleased. 'Get me a lager, there's a good girl, Barbara.'

Bibi stood up.

'And yourself . . . yourself something. On second thoughts, I think I'll just have a lime juice. I seem to be putting on weight.'

He looked angrily down at his waist.

'What nonsense, Maurice, you're just imagining it. A gin and tonic for me, dear.'

'The bathroom scales have no imagination. I'm putting it on somewhere and at any moment, if I'm not careful, I may become a fat man. Definitely lime juice.'

'Constance? Anything for you?' asked Bibi, moving away towards the house.

'No thanks.'

'Ice. Don't forget ice in my gin. Constance wants to leave college, Maurice.'

'Oh, why?'

Father sounded fairly uninterested.

Constance pulled a long hair out of the top of her head and wound it round a finger.

'I want to go away.'

'I've told her she should wait and get her degree first. It seems silly . . .'

'I have always considered a degree in English and French to be of dubious benefit. I presume Constance has come to the same conclusion. Better late than never.'

'She wants to go away.'

Constance unwound the hair from her finger and dropped it on the grass.

'Did you have anything specific in mind?'

'I thought I'd . . . well . . . London perhaps. I've got the money granny left me. I wouldn't need . . .'

'You shouldn't just go spending that,' said Mother angrily.

Father waved a hand in her direction.

'Or Paris perhaps . . .'

'There are problems like exchange control and labour permits.'

'Anyway I'd like to try London first. See what happens.'

'What do you expect to happen?'

She blushed suddenly.

'I don't know. I'd like to try . . . and . . . well, write . . . but I . . .'

He looked at her with a glimmer of interest.

'Write?'

'I don't suppose . . .'

'Write.'

He rubbed at his waist with his hand for a moment, trying to shift the unwanted flesh.

Mother laughed.

Mother's laugh had always been musical, neatly controlled.

'What on earth do you know about writing? Goodness gracious, even your school compositions weren't up to much.'

'Write,' repeated Father. There was a green stain on his tennis flannels, just below the knee. 'Ah, yes. No harm in trying. Mind you,' he smiled suddenly in Constance's direction, not at her, but towards her. 'The world is full of unpublished . . . or rather I should say, the dustbins of the world are full of unpublished novels. Was it novels you had in mind?'

Constance blushed again and nodded.

'Really, Maurice, I don't think you should be encouraging . . .'

'I neither encourage, nor discourage. As long as Constance doesn't expect me to finance her folly, she is at liberty to do what she wishes with her life. It is after all, her life.'

Mother looked very put out.

'She's only a child still.'

'The quickest and easiest way to cure that particular sickness is to throw yourself, alone and unprotected upon the world.'

'Why do you have to go to London to write? Why can't you write here?'

'I want to go.'

'She wants to go.' Father smiled again as he spoke the words. Bibi clinked across the grass towards them with a tray of glasses and floating cubes of ice.

'It's utterly idiotic.'

'What's up?'

Bibi handed Father his glass of lime. She had taken the liberty of putting ice into it also.

'Constance is being idiotic,' said Mother.

'Nothing new. Here. Tell me if it's okay.'

Mother sipped.

'Lovely, dear.'

'So, what have you done this time?' asked Bibi.

'She wants to go and write novels in London.'

Bibi laughed.

'Typical. Daft. Oh, silly Constance, you'll come to a sticky end.'

'Shut up.'

Father got up from his deck-chair.

'Well,' he said, 'I think I'll go and have a bath. I'm dining at the Club. Bridge.' He looked vaguely down the garden at the tennis court. He took a couple of steps towards Constance and put out a hand and touched her shoulder. The hand fluttered away immediately as if he had committed some slight sin.

'When are you leaving?'

'Well, not just yet . . . I've hardly had time to . . .'

'Maurice . . .'

'Don't go without saying goodbye.'

He walked off towards the house, the glass of lime juice tinkling in one hand, leaving his tennis racquet for Bibi to put away.

✳   ✳   ✳

The bell was cracked and the sound raw. Starlings scattered upwards from the trees, complaining for a few moments and then sank once more down through the leaves to recommence their evening's drowsy twittering. Half the piazza was golden, and the curving harbour wall was washed by gold tipped waves, the café was in the deep shade, comfortably warm, an auditorium.

For a moment Constance watched the birds, no one else seemed to be affected by the bell, no one visibly turned their thoughts towards God. The man at the table to her right put down the pen with which he had been writing in a notebook and put out his hand for his glass. Constance crossed the first two fingers of her right hand. He turned to look for the waiter and caught Constance's eye. He smiled slightly, acknowledging their mutual foreignness. She smiled back and pressed the twisted fingers tightly together.

As the waiter made his way towards them through the tables, everyone was startled by a rustle of wind. Hats were whisked from heads, skirts lifted, over-used lira notes whirled from table tops and around Constance's feet blew the loose pages from someone's notebook. She stopped and picked them up, seven, eight closely scribbled pages. Black crawling insects on the white paper. She put the sheets on the table in front of her and patted them together. Jumbled, incomprehensible words in what seemed like several languages. Heavy scoring lines. Xs. He seemed very hot on Xs.

'Thank you,' said a voice.

She felt her face going red. She looked up. He was standing beside her, looking down, with a smile on his face.

'I wasn't reading it. Honestly I wasn't.' She laughed suddenly. 'I couldn't anyway. You must admit, no one could read that.'

He took the papers from her and fitted them neatly into the notebook that he now held in his hand. Sleek black hair covered the backs of his arms, growing right down to his knuckles. A gorilla, she thought. She imagined the rug of black hair that must cover him from his shoulders right down to his waist. It would be handy in the winter, save on the heating bills. An urban gorilla. The waiter appeared beside them.

'Signor?'

'Una bottiglia di bianco. Vino bianco. Grazie . . . oh and due bicchieri, glasses. Capisce?'

The waiter was used to it all and nodded. He picked up the empty glass from the table, made a flourish with a little red cloth and went back towards the café. The man turned to Constance.

'You'll have a drink?'

She gestured towards the empty chair at her table and he sat down. His fingers fidgeted for a moment with the notebook.

'Sometimes I can't read it either. I have to struggle for a long time. Counter-productive, I think I could call it.'

She wondered what to say.

'I . . .'

He leaned his elbows on the table and looked her up and down.

'You have a name.'

A statement.

'Constance Keating. I come from Dublin. Ireland that is. I'm not English. Everyone thinks I'm English. They take it for granted. I just thought I'd make that clear.'

He smiled slightly.

'You've made it clear. Do you, perhaps, have a natural antipathy towards the British?'

'Permesso.'

The waiter came between them and placed two glasses and a bottle on the table.

'Oh no. I didn't mean that. It's just . . . well most people think we're the same thing . . . you know . . . Irish, English . . . I suppose it's because we use the same language. All lumped together in one mass. I suppose it's silly to get annoyed. Of course it is, but I've lived among the English so long that . . . well, I've become very aware of the differences. Where's your brogue? they ask me, really not believing me. All Irish people speak incomprehensibly and poetically, are dirty, violent and probably have pigs in the kitchen. Not quite up to the mark, you know? I just like them to know where they stand, right away. I don't ever want to be accused of trying to pass. I don't mean to be aggressive.'

He smiled slightly. He filled the two glasses with wine from the bottle.

'I hope you don't mind drinking the white? I have trabble with my stomach. I must not drink the red. The doctors say that to me. No red.'

'I like white.'

He took a sip and then nodded at the glass with approval.

'I,' he said, in a somewhat mournful voice, 'am happy to be British.'

She burst out laughing.

'Why you laugh?'

'I'm sorry. I didn't mean to be rude. But your voice is so un-British . . . you look so . . .'

'What do I look?'

'Foreign.'

'I am British.'

He leaned across the table towards her, the glass raised in his hand.

'Swoboda.'

'What's that, British person?'

'Freedom, Irish woman. Britain gave me that present.'

She lifted her glass and replied ironically to his toast.

'Swoboda.'

They drank.

'My name is Jacob Weinberg.'

He ducked his head towards her as he spoke.

'A good old British name.'

'I see you are a person who laughs at things a lot. Chokes.'

'Yes. I prefer it that way.'

'I am a Chew.'

'Mmmm.'

'And too, Polish.'

'Oh . . . ah . . . yes . . . I . . .'

'But since a long time I have been British. Now you understand my situation?'

'Yes, of course . . . I . . .'

'I have come to Britain when I was sixteen. A child. Thirty years ago, and I still can't speak the language right.' He laughed, opening his mouth wide and throwing his head back.

Not a bit British that laugh, she thought.

'You see what a poor fish I am.' He hitched his chair nearer to the table, nearer to her. 'A poor fish. And I am a writer. Now you know all there is to know. Me voilà.' He took another drink and stared at her.

'A writer?'

'You don't mind?'

'Why should I mind? I have a close acquaintanceship with many writers.'

'You have?'

'Mostly dead.'

He laughed.

'Should I . . . should . . . ?'

'Only by accident do people read my books. It is not likely that such an accident should have happened to you.'

'I read a lot.'

'Dead people.'

'I'm catching up. Maybe I'll get to you one day if, as they say at home, I'm spared.'

'I write fanny books. Sometimes I even laugh myself at them. Short, fanny. People read them by accident and then they laugh. They look then to the next one coming. That is good.'

'You make lots of money?'

'I make ends meet. I have trabbles with language . . . grammar. That is crazy for a writer. You have to admit that is a little crazy.'

'Well, yes, it would be difficult.'

'You see, inside me the Polish language and my Yiddish are drying up. I have no longer ease with them . . . to manipulate. And English . . .' He sighed comically and rolled his eyes, whirled them like some Uncle Sambo on the screen. 'I have always the trabbles with the grammar. Always. I am a poor fish.'

She laughed.

'It sounds like you've chosen the wrong career.'

'There was no choosing,' he said.

There was a long silence between them. The laughter and noise of the crowds formed a wall around their silence. She looked at her hands, fingers laced in stillness on the table in front of her and wondered if he had said all he was going to say, if their silence would last for ever.

'You have no shadows on your face,' he said at last. 'You have the face of a nun. A well-protected face.'

She looked at him and smiled faintly. His own face was well shadowed, his eyes nonetheless tranquil.

'I tell you what we do, Irish woman, when we have finished our wine we will go and eat fish. You like fish? Here there is nothing to eat but fish and pasta. Pasta and fish on and on. And melanzane. I like meat. When first I get to London and see the meat, I nearly went crazy. And then there was rations, but still, crazy. I could stand outside those shop windows and look at meat for hours. But for a few weeks in Italy I can do without meat. What you say? I talk too much. I see you thinking that. It is true. I talk too much. What you say?'

'I like fish and pasta and melanzane . . . but . . .'

'No but. We will get a little drunk, which is good from time to time and eat what we like and then we will go to bed, which is also good. What you say?'

He leant across the table and touched her hand with a finger.

'Hunh?'

'Yes.'

'Good. More wine. I like a woman to know her mind.'

*　*　*

Bibi had come into the house. I could hear her in the kitchen moving things around. She was one of those women who always had to move things around in other people's kitchens. She couldn't believe that anyone might be anything other than delighted by her re-arrangements. I drained the dregs from my glass and dropped the empty bottle in the wastepaper basket.

I walked across the hall and into the kitchen. She was unwrapping little parcels of food and putting them into the fridge; a china bowl full of soup, half a quiche, two yoghurts and three tomatoes in a transparent plastic bag.

'Oh, hello. You're very bright and early. Hello, hello.'

Over-enthusiastic, you cow.

She turned and looked at me. A red and blue silk scarf was knotted just on the point of her chin, her coat was dark polished, mink, her bag and gloves sat neatly on the table beside the tomatoes.

'You've been cleaning up.'

43

I nodded.

'I hope you haven't overdone things.'

She picked up the tomatoes and put them on the bottom shelf of the fridge.

'It's all a great improvement. It really was a pig sty before. You're looking better too. Taken a pull out of yourself. Marvellous. Washed your hair?'

'What's left of it.'

'Never mind, dear. It's a step . . .' She stopped talking and looked at me again. 'Marvellous.'

'I feel great. I could go dancing, or climb a mountain . . . lots of things like that. Will you take me into town?'

Bibi shut the fridge door carefully.

'What on earth do you want to go into town for?'

'I want to see it all. It's been so long since I've been here at Christmas. I want to see the lights in Grafton Street, nostalgia things . . . you know. Have a drink in the Hibernian, listen to the carol singers, smell all those lovely rich Christmas smells. Just remember.'

'Nothing's the same as it used to be.'

'And get some presents.'

'Nobody wants presents, Constance. Don't be silly. It's a perfectly dreadful day. Even walking from the gate I was drenched. Nobody wants presents. When the weather gets better you can buy us all presents then, if you insist.'

'When the weather gets better . . .' I stopped. No point in making her cross. 'I can have a big hot bath when I get home. I do want to go Bibi . . . really I do.'

'There's a quiche in the fridge and some soup. They just need heating up, that's all. I put a Vienna loaf in the bread crock and there's lots of fruit. Is there anything else you'd like? I'll be back this afternoon.'

'Take me into town.'

'Ah, Constance, have a bit of wit. Look, tomorrow if the sun is shining I'll take you to the Glen of the Downs, or somewhere. How would that be? A nice drive. If the sun . . .'

I didn't say anything. There wasn't much point.

'How nice that dress looks on you. It's good to see you . . . well . . . making some effort. If you give me some of your clothes I'll get Miss Green to take them in for you. Actually, I'm sure she'd come round, that would be best of all.'

'I prefer pins.'

'Have it your own way. I must fly. What about a quick cup of coffee before I go? Or some hot chocolate? A cup of hot chocolate, wouldn't that be nice?'

'No thanks.'

'Did you have any breakfast?'

'I wasn't hungry.'

'You must try to eat something, Constance. Just a little. It's most important. Eat some lunch. There's no point in us cooking things for you and you just letting them go bad in the fridge, is there?'

I shook my head.

'And you've been drinking again. I can smell it.'

'So, I've been drinking? I don't try to hide it.'

Bibi picked up the right glove from the table and pulled it on, smoothing the black leather over her fingers.

'People only want to help you.'

'I know.' I tried to make my voice as humble as I could. 'I'm so grateful to you . . .'

She began to massage on the second glove.

'No one wants gratitude. You know that . . . we just want you to help us help you. That's all. I must say you've cleaned the place up very nicely. I really must fly. Would you like Charles to come round this evening and see you?'

'No.'

She looked slightly relieved.

'The child is settling down nicely. I think your decision not to see her is right. We wouldn't want her to get upset. Confused.'

Silent pause.

'I'll be seeing Sister Aloysius later this morning . . . about a girl.'

'Oh yes . . . thank you.'

Polite smiles.

'The children are dying to see you. They'll be round as soon as . . .'

'Yes.'

'So.'

'So.'

'Au revoir, dear. Don't overdo things . . . and try and . . . not too much to drink.'

'Tra la.'

Her shiny boots marched across the hall and out of the door.

＊　＊　＊

They hadn't come to see her off; neither Mother, nor Father, nor even Bibi. It was common sense really when you thought about it, prolonged leavetakings were made uneasy by the demands of moderate behaviour.

Constance had been screwing the top on the toothpaste when there had been a knock on her bedroom door. She picked a glob of dry paste off the top of the tube and dropped it into the basin.

'Come in.'

Her father opened the door and stood on the threshold, looking around the room with a certain interest.

'Come in. Come in, do. I was just . . .'

'Don't let me disturb you.'

He was dressed in a brown tweed suit. She remembered he was off to the country for the weekend.

'You're not. It's just the last few things. I'm . . .' She gestured with the toothpaste.

'I won't come in,' he said sternly, as if he were taking some moral stand or other. 'You're all right? You've got your tickets and all that sort of thing? Money? Got enough money for the journey?' He cleared his throat.

'Yes thank you, Father. I'm fine. I'm terribly highly organised. Bill is bringing me to the boat.'

'Bill. Yes. Good. Bill.'

He wore his father's gold watch chain across the front of his waistcoat and now, for something to do, he pulled the watch from his pocket and looked down at it cradled in his hand.

'Time getting on. I'm afraid . . .'

'I'll be all right, Father.'

'Yes.'

He slipped the watch back into his pocket. Smooth and old and warm it had always been when he had allowed her to touch it.

'Yes. If I come over to London, I'll let you know.'

'Yes. Do that.'

'Give you a meal. You'll probably need a square meal.'

They both laughed.

'If you . . . ah . . . ah write anything good, you might send me a copy.'

'Yes.'

'Right then. I must be off. I have to pick up Henry LeClerc. We're driving down to . . . Goodbye.'

He held out his hand towards her.

'Goodbye, Father.'

She walked across the room towards him, the toothpaste still in her hand. She kissed his right, slightly scented cheek. He looked surprised, but not altogether displeased.

'Try,' he said, and turned abruptly and walked across the landing.

'Goodbye,' she called after him.

Later on Mother had taken the car and gone out to dinner. She had always hated stations and docks and Woolworths, places like that where hundreds of people didn't care who they pushed or bumped against. Her disapproval lasted up to the very last moment.

'I expect we'll see you back soon,' were her last words as she left the house.

Bibi didn't even telephone.

'I'll carry your case on board for you.'

'No thanks, Bill. It's not heavy.'

'We could have a quick drink.'

'No. Thank you all the same. I'd rather not. I might get all emotional.'

'Not you.'

'Embarkations tend to be emotional.'

He gave a short laugh and opened the door of the car for her. Dry dung blew around their feet. Seagulls mewed above the black roofs. Expectant smoke drifted with the gulls on the slight wind.

'You'll have a good crossing,' said Bill.

He pulled the brown leather case out of the back of the car.

'You travel light.'

'There wasn't much I wanted to bring.'

'Perhaps you'll be back soon?'

'That's what Mother said. I'm never coming back.'

'Silly.'

'Goodbye, Bill.' She kissed him.

Sawdust and straw danced in the little safe breeze.

'And thank you. Thanks for everything.'

'Goodbye, Constance.'

'Love to Angela Dillon.'

He blushed furiously and she felt mean.

'Sorry. I shouldn't have said that. I really wish you all the . . .'

'Oh shut up,' said Bill and got into the car and slammed the door.

As she put her foot on the first step of the gangway she thought, this is it, miss. This is it. This is it.

* * *

In the cloakroom there was a pair of old fur-lined boots. Bald patches on the brown suede gave them a somewhat diseased look. My mother must have bought them at some stage during the war, when to keep warm was more important than to look elegant. I buried my feet in them and hoped that I would be able to retain some sort of control over their movements. I walked experimentally round the cloakroom and then courageously strode up and down the hall. All seemed well, if they had once been seven leaguers, their magic days were behind them. I was in no danger of being whisked over and around the four provinces at the twitch of a toe. I put on my tweed coat and belted it tightly round my waist, then a woollie cap. I couldn't find my gloves. You can never find gloves when you really want them, unless like Bibi you imprison them in boxes and drawers, keep them under lock and key.

The snow had stopped but the east wind was still blowing bitterly. The front garden was as neat as it had always been. The beds under their dust of snow were raked and waiting for spring. Bibi's gardener came round once a week and trimmed and weeded, cut the grass and raked the gravel path, cut back the creeper from the basement windows and cleared the gutters before they became choked with leaves. Tuesday was his day. He never impinged upon my solitude. He took his cup of tea and two digestive biscuits from me at the kitchen door, nodding

his silent gratitude and disappearing with them to the wooden shed
in the back garden where the tools were kept. Before he left he would
leave the mug, with its pattern of tea leaves streaking up one side and
the tiny residue of sugar in the bottom, and the silver spoon and the
plate neatly on the shelf just inside the kitchen door. If I were there,
visible, he would nod once more towards me, that was all. Two nods
a week for five or six weeks had been the sum total of our
communication. The back garden had been let go since Father's death.
The fruit trees remained unpruned, the tennis court was shaggy with
uncut grass and weeds, moss was creeping over the paths. It was
important though, said Bibi, with the prospect of the house being
on the market in the not too distant future, that the front garden be
kept up to the mark.

The iron railings down the steps were chilling to my ungloved
hands. Damn, bloody gloves. I stood just inside the gate watching the
cars move past. Fans of muddy water spread out from under their
wheels. The pavement was caked with dirty snow. The clouds were
green and pressing down towards the city with the weight of more
snow. The wind sliced through my tweed coat and my cardigan and
the blue pinned dress and my perished skin and made me shiver. The
bravado I had felt as I strutted round the hall had gone and I felt
afraid suddenly. I wasn't quite sure why I was afraid. It was all so
familiar. The terraced houses, the neat hedges, the silver street-lamps,
the urban trees. Familiar. Home. When I had closed my eyes in
London I had seen these granite steps, felt the eternal trembling as
the cars moved past, smelt the green hedges and the dust and the
garden fires of raked leaves. Familiar. My safety. Had been. Twelve
steps up to the front door and then through the letterbox you could
see a rectangular segment of the floor, table legs, red welcoming
carpet and the polished shoes coming towards you. All that was so
long ago and now the clouds were pressing down, the clipped hedges,

winter bare, moved imperceptibly towards me. The houses' eyes stared. From under the wheels of the cars the water fanned up and up. You could drown, I thought. I held the top of the gate tight in case the wind should blow me under the wheels of the cars, into the fanning water.

'Paranoia.'

I said it aloud. I must have said it very loud, as a man who had been standing at the bus stop turned and looked at me. He looked cold. He looked as though he had been there a long time. He looked anxiously at me as if maybe he thought I was going to create some new problem for him.

'Par . . . a . . . noi . . . a.'

The boots felt heavy as I walked back along the path and up the twelve steps to the hall door. The effort of lifting each weighted foot from step to step made my heart feel as if it were going to burst inside me.

It wasn't until I had the door firmly closed behind me that the fear began to drain away, leaving me cold and very very tired. I sat down carefully in one of the chairs by the door. It hadn't really been an inspirational outing.

Trams had been so beautiful, rocking like tall ships on their silver rails. The shoe shop had always given you a balloon, red, blue, choose your own colour, yellow, like a moon on its long string. The wind tugged at it as you crossed the road, running the last few steps to avoid the cars, holding tight to Nanny's hand, the other hand holding even tighter the dancing moon. It could escape, fly up, free, blown by the wind around the whole world, or up to join its sister way, way up, or just come to a sticky end on the high railings around College Park. Or burst in the tram. That had happened once and I had cried. Nanny had taken her white folded handkerchief out of the pocket of her coat and wiped my eyes and 'Look,' she had said, 'Look,' and pointed up an evening street lined with high houses and there at the end of the street the mountains rose, the outside world and behind them the sun was going down, a gold balloon falling into the darkness behind the hills.

'Will it ever come up again?' I had asked her, thinking I suppose, of my balloon.

'Yes, pet. It'll come up. It will always come up. Even when there's big black clouds and you can't see it. It's up there going round and round forever.'

It was years before I could be persuaded to believe the heretical truth.

I laughed at that shadow of the past.

'I thought I'd given those boots to the tinkers.'

Mother stood at the bottom of the stairs, her hand on the curl at the bottom of the banisters. I could see the flash of her rings as her fingers moved.

'I certainly meant to. Hideous things. I only bought them the year we thought we weren't going to get coal ever again. We had to use that awful turf. Hopeless. Wherever did you find them?'

'In the cloakroom. There's a lot of peculiar things in the cloakroom. Forgotten items.'

'What are you doing sitting there anyway, all huddled up like that?'

'I was thinking about trams.'

'You look as if you are ill. Are you ill?'

'Yes, Mother.'

'Why trams? There haven't been any trams for years. What a curious thing to be thinking about.'

'Sometimes you can't help odd things storming into your head.'

'You were always perfectly healthy as a child. Apart from those tiresome things like measles and chickenpox. Bibi was susceptible to bronchitis, but you were never ill. I don't remember you ever being ill.'

She looked at me with curiosity.

'What's the matter with you?'

'I have cancer, Mother.'

She turned away from me abruptly and walked towards the kitchen door. 'I'd like to have had a son.'

She made it sound as if, somehow, it were my fault that she hadn't.

'I have very few regrets. That is one of them.'

She looked back towards me over her shoulder.

'Cancer, you say?'

'Yes.'

'Strange. No one in the family has ever had that before.'

'But . . .'

There seemed no point in saying the obvious.

'There has to be a first time for everything!' I said instead.

'You always had to be difficult.'

I laughed. The hall was empty. I was shivering. I got to my feet and went to look for the whiskey bottle. The water of life.

*   *   *

Bill brought the tree.

I was sitting at my little table by the fire trying to concentrate, to gather my wandering thoughts, to mould together the images pressing into the front of my mind and the words that gave them some sort of meaning.

'Typing, I see.'

He came into the room carrying the tree in front of him. The beautiful smell of pine needles filled the room.

'You see what an obedient animal I am. As ordered, one tree.'

He put it down on the floor and we had a look at it. A good

compact tree, neat, no straggling branches. Just the tree I would have chosen myself. He had wedged it into a round brass pot.

'It's lovely. Really lovely. Thank you, Bill.'

'Where will I put it?'

'On that table there in the window. You are good. I hope it wasn't too much bother.'

'What on earth are you wearing those peculiar clothes for?'

I realised I was still dressed in the boots and overcoat.

'Oh . . .'

'I hope you weren't thinking of going out. I would be very, very angry if you did a silly thing like that.'

'I just put them on for fun.'

'A likely tale. Ooops.'

He lifted the tree on to the table.

'Doesn't that look marvellous? Have you got decorations and all that?'

'Somewhere. I'll look later. I feel terribly excited. If I were still at school, I'd write an essay called My Last Christmas Tree.'

He laughed.

'Dreadful woman.'

'Will you have a cup of coffee? I haven't the foggiest idea what the time is.'

'No, thanks. I'm doing my rounds, and everything's a bit hectic. Sit down and let me take those things off your feet.'

I sat down. Gently he pulled off each boot and stood them side by side on the floor.

'You looked as if you were going to drown in them. You must have energy today. Typing, drowning in boots, you've even cleaned the place up a bit. What are you typing, or shouldn't I ask?'

I leaned back in the chair and looked at the tree.

'I thought maybe I could sort a few things out for myself.

I've always been led to believe that an awareness . . .'

In the Pine Forest it had been so silent that you could hear the needles slithering to the ground, the distant musical whisper of water.

'Awareness?'

He was rubbing bark stain off one of his hands with his handkerchief.

'I thought that the urgency of it all might make my mind clear. Show me a pattern of some sort. "Depend upon it, sir, when a man knows he is to be hanged in a fortnight, it concentrates his mind wonderfully." One great saying proved wrong. I find myself lost in a forest of irrelevancies.'

'You're not going to be hanged in a fortnight.'

'Don't let's be too literal about it.'

'Who said that anyway? It's vaguely familiar.'

'I don't really remember. You'd better go and look after your patients. The flu, the measles and the problems of the lower back. I will decorate the tree. Tomorrow you can come and admire it . . . and give yourself time to stay and have a drink.'

'Yes. I'll do that. Can I get your slippers or something to put on your feet.'

'I'm all right.'

'The floor is cold.'

'I'll get them later. You run along.'

He touched my shoulder with a finger. A few small green needles from the tree clung to the sleeve of his coat.

'Thank you, Bill.'

*   *   *

Jacob Weinberg had two small rooms on the first floor of a house overlooking the bay. A narrow road ran between the houses and the stony beach, filled in the daytime with a constant chaos of small motorised vehicles equipped with horns of the most varied ingenuity and resonance. At night it was silent. The sea sighed over the stones and the starlings in the branches of the trees sometimes twittered in their sleep. Constance stood on the balcony and looked across the road at the sea. The street lamps seemed to grow like flowers through the oleanders. Three or four boats were pulled up on to the stones and out in the bay the lights from three or four others could be seen shining into the blackness of the water, enticing the fish to the surface. The voices of the fishermen drifted across the water. The romance of it all is unbearable, she thought. Unbearable. She went back into the room. He was standing by the table pouring wine into a glass. For the first time she noticed his hands, the joints knotted, disfigured, like the hands of an old man.

'I have to say something.'

She walked over to the table and stood staring into his face.

He nodded.

'Go ahead.'

'I have never done this before.'

He pushed the glass of wine across the table towards her.

'Sit down, Irish woman. Relex. It is important to relex. I have done it before. I like it. You, too, will like it.'

Obediently, she sat down. He pulled another chair up to the table and sat down facing her.

'Drink,' he ordered.

They both drank. He stared at her over the rim of his glass.

'Why?' he asked eventually.

'I suppose I was wrong . . . oh I know I've been wrong all the way down the line. It seemed so simple years ago when I left home. I just wanted to be free. Totally free. I wanted to find out whatever it was I had to find out in my own way, at my own speed. Not be . . . well . . . beholden. I had hoped . . .'

She looked at him. His eyes were shut, the lids were like pale shells in the darkness of the sockets, strange, like as if the sun, or even the air had never touched them.

'. . . to write. Be a writer. But it was hopeless. I was hopeless. I suppose I didn't have anything to say. Not enough talent . . . perhaps no purpose. It could have been that.'

'Who said it was hopeless?'

His eyes were still shut.

'I knew. I sold a few stories here and there, but they were wrong. No gut somehow. No voice.'

The light floating in the red glasses. Stars.

'You have to find a voice. Perhaps. . . .'

She raised the star-filled glass.

'I am not very good at expressing myself.'

He smiled, eyes open now.

'You haven't answered my question.'

'Oh that. I always thought that it would get in the way. That sort of involvement with people clouds the issue. You're always having to adjust your thoughts to accommodate . . . I don't think it's quite the same for a man. They are somehow so . . . indomitable.'

'Had you no curiosity even?'

'I had that. Yes. But I saw so much anguish. It seemed best just to leave it all alone. I think I'm just a selfish . . . bastard. Yes, I think it probably boils down to that. Eternally protecting myself against any possibility of pain.'

'So, what made you change your mind?'

She paused a moment, bending her head once more towards her glass.

'I haven't changed my mind. I don't want to set up a great chain reaction of relationships and responsibilities. I just want to find out what sex feels like, does to me, before it's too late.'

He laughed.

'So you pick on me? I am glad you pick on me, Irish woman. Tomorrow we will go to your hotel and pick up your luggage and you will come and stay here.'

'Oh no . . . I . . .'

He splashed some more wine into their glasses.

'Have you a wife?' she asked, after a long silence.

'I have no one. Nothing. Since a long time I have had no one.' He ran one of his distorted fingers round the rim of his glass.

'Since the war.'

'I'm sorry.'

'No need to say sorry. Sorry is only a word. If you say it over and over it becomes a word that means nothing. A mumbo jumbo. Too many people have been sorry.'

He stretched his hands out across the table. She stared at them.

'Are you frightened of my hands?'

He turned them over so that she had to stare at the palms, savaged by deep sad lines.

'No.'

She put her right hand out and laid it in the palm of his.

'There is no need for fear. They are ugly . . . yes. Ugly. But they have survived. There is an honour in survival. Yes?'

He closed his fingers over hers.

'What happened?'

She didn't know whether she should ask or not.

'They broke my fingers. And those bones that run there . . . there. I do not know what they are called. Yes. Those ones. I was lucky. They could have killed me like they killed the others. They chose to break my fingers first . . . a sort of hors d'oeuvre perhaps. Then, it was too late to kill me. It was all over. I think perhaps they weren't going to kill me at all. My father had been a musician, and maybe they thought I might have had ideas of being one too. You can't really be a very good musician if your fingers don't work. But they were wrong about me. I can play the typewriter.'

He laughed.

'They really should have killed me too.'

He rubbed at the back of her hand with his thumb.

'Now I begin to get arthritis. That is not very agreeable . . .'

'I . . .'

'What is strange to me is that I know . . . even now . . . I can tell . . . today if one of them comes into a room, a restaurant, a bar. I know. My whole body starts to shake. My hands first and then my whole body. There is nothing I can do to stop it. Why do I shake, I ask myself, like as if I has some fever, and I start to look around. I see then a young man, an old man. Maybe a beautiful girl. It makes no difference. I do not even need to hear her voice. I must then go. It is something inside me, some animal thing that I cannot control. And with my mind I could not say that I hate them. It is a fear about which I can do nothing. Nothing.'

She pulled her hand away from his and stood up.

'I'm cold.'

'Poor Irish, how dismal I am being.'

He got up and walked around the table to her. He put his arms around her, pulled her close to his warmth.

'It will be good. Believe. It will be good.'

*　　*　　*

I found the decorations in a blue wooden box, just as I had remembered them, in a cupboard in the far corner of the cloakroom. The cupboard door hadn't been opened for years and had swollen slightly with the damp, and I had to go to the kitchen to fetch a knife with which to lever the wood, scrape off little flakes of decaying paint. The smell of dust and dead mice and dried up rubber boots hit me as the door finally swung open. My father's fishing gear was neatly stacked, just as he had put it away after he had last used it. His Hardy rods and the nets, leaning against the wall, all sorts of canvas bags and fly boxes tidily on the shelf, his waders, part of the source of the smell on the floor, below the hook on which hung an oilskin jacket, so dry now that it looked as though it would disintegrate into dust if you were to touch it. Not that I wanted to touch it, nor anything else connected with it. We had never been allowed to disturb in any way my father's belongings. I felt guilty enough about my abuse of his study without tempting reproof of some sort from him by moving his fishing tackle.

A long wooden box, like a small coffin, held the croquet mallets and the balls. The hoops and posts were under the bottom shelf, in need of a good coat of paint. Several tennis racquets needed to be thrown out. Bibi could sort it all out one day. Sending some things to charitable organisations, selling others and keeping some on the chance that sometime there would be a use for them again. Two hockey sticks . . . what a sporting lot we must have been . . . and a lacrosse stick, some walking sticks and a pair of skates. My mother's garden hat was on the shelf in front of the door and beside it her wooden trug, with a pair of secateurs sitting placidly in it. The whole damn cupboard had a Sleeping Beauty feeling about it that made me feel uneasy.

A British army greatcoat hung from a hook on the wall. It must have belonged to my grandfather. It was surprising that the moths hadn't devoured it in all those years, or the mice. Behind it I found the blue wooden box, neatly covered by several dusty sheets of newspaper. I took it out into the hall and wedged the cupboard door shut again. Shutting in the must and the passive ghosts. There was a plug at the end of the fairy lights. I switched it on and sat back in my chair to look at them. To rest. They didn't give me the thrill that they had given me as a child. There was no expectant rapture. They looked old and tired and very unglamorous, just as I felt. I had no energy left and lay back in the chair staring at the lights and willing my heart to go on beating. I heard the hall door open and Bibi's footsteps crossed the hall. As usual she went into the kitchen, checking up on me. I smiled. Her feet crossed the hall and she came into the room.

'Comme c'est beau,' she said, stopping in the doorway. 'Constance? Ah, Constance. Lovely dear. I hope you haven't overdone things.'

'I hate those lights. Will you get me a string of those tiny ones, like little pearls? Those are so old-fashioned and sort of sleazy. The sort of lights you see in church halls.'

'I think they're lovely. Don't you think they're lovely?'

She switched on the light and we blinked at each other. A small dark girl stood just behind her.

'I can never understand why you sit in the dark. You look all washed out. You've done too much. I'll make us all a cup of tea. This is Bridie. You're very, very lucky, my dear, she'd be prepared to stay for a month or so. If you both like each other, that is, of course. Give a hand. See to things. I'll go and put the kettle on and you can both have a little chat.'

She left the room abruptly and the girl and I stared at each other in silence.

'Hello, Bridie,' I said eventually. 'Won't you sit down?'

'Thank you, miss.'

She walked calmly across the room and sat down in the armchair on the other side of the fire.

'Don't you think that smaller lights would be better?'

She looked at the tree before answering.

A long, careful look.

'I saw a tree once had nothing but wee blue lights on it. All over. Nothing but blue. It looked smashing.'

'What a good idea. I'll ask Bibi to get me a string of blue lights. Are you a nurse?'

The girl shook her head.

'No, miss. I'm an orphan.'

I laughed. A slight smile moved her mouth.

'So am I, if it comes to that.'

'I don't mean like you, miss. I've been in the home all my life. I've worked there the last three years. They've been very good to me. Mrs Barry's known me since I was a child. Since I was ... she's always been very good to me.'

'And now you want to get out?'

'Well ...'

She paused for a long time, staring at the flames and the dancing sparks that scattered up into the darkness of the chimney.

'They've all been ...'

'Very good to you.'

'Yes, miss.'

She looked towards me now, judging, weighing me up.

'What are you thinking of doing when you leave here? You won't be here very long, you know.'

'I thought I'd go to England.'

'Why England?'

'I thought it would make a change, miss. A lot of the girls go over there. No one knows about you there. Anyway ...'

'Anyway?'

She just shrugged and looked away from me, back towards the fire again.

'Has Bibi told you about me?'

'She's told me you're not very well, miss. That's all really.'

I smiled.

'I don't want to be looked after.'

'I'll do whatever you tell me, miss. I'm good at that. Mrs Barry'll tell you. I've been well trained.'

'I don't want to be called miss, for a start. Constance is my name. Okay?'

'Okay.'

She nodded. She might have been smiling, but it was hard to tell.

'Why would you consider coming here anyway? It won't be the most cheerful of jobs. Hanging round a cranky bitch like me. Waiting for the worst to happen.'

'The money's good. What Mrs Barry offered me was good, and then my keep. I'll need a few bob in my pocket when I get to London. If I worked in a restaurant or a shop I'd have to spend all I earned on living. I doubt I'd even save the fare.'

'You have it all worked out?'

'Yes.'

'If I asked you to do some writing for me . . . would you mind that? You know, if I dictated . . . something like that? You see the time may come when I'm not able to do it for myself. I hope not, but you never know.'

'I could do that. I'm very good at spelling. I was the best at spelling in the school.'

'That's great.'

Bibi bumped the door open with the tea tray and came into the room.

'Everything fixed up?'

'It's up to Bridie really. I'm happy. But I don't suppose she has the foggiest idea what she's taking on.'

'I explained . . .'

'Explaining never means a thing.'

'I'd like to come,' said the girl.

'Tea. Tea, Bridie? Constance? I got a Bewley's brack when I was in town. I know how much you like it.'

I took the plate she handed me and put it on the table. I broke a small piece of brack and put it in my mouth. Bibi put a cup of tea down beside the plate. I chewed.

'That's splendid. All settled then. I'll bring her round tomorrow and her things. Sister Aloysius will be pleased that things have worked out so well. If you take sugar, Bridie, help yourself. Have a piece of brack.'

I couldn't swallow the food. My throat had closed completely. I took a drink of tea and tried to force the moist crumbs down the back of my throat.

'She has to eat something,' said Bibi, nodding her head in my direction. 'The doctor says she must eat.'

Bridie munched at her brack but didn't say a word.

'If you would get me some lights for the tree . . .'

'Those ones look marvellous.'

'What colour did you say, Bridie?'

'Blue,' said Bridie.

'Blue please, Bibi. Tiny little blue ones.'

'Donald comes home from Downside tomorrow.'

'If you can't find blue, gold might be nice. What do you think, Bridie?'

She nodded.

'I have to meet him at the airport. Two-thirty I think the plane gets in.'

'Perhaps Bridie could get them for me and bring them with her tomorrow? Would that be possible?'

'I could do that all right. I'd like a run into town.'

'I'll give you some money.'

'I'll be all right. I have enough. I'll tell you what you owe me.'

'I wouldn't really have time to take you for a drive tomorrow afternoon. By the time I get back from the airport and get Donald his lunch . . .'

'That's all right, Bibi, don't worry about it.'

'Perhaps the next day, if the weather improves.'

'That would be lovely.'

'Yes. That's everything arranged. Bridie, take that tray into the kitchen and leave it on the table. We must get on our way.' Obediently Bridie gathered up the cups and plates on to the tray and left the room.

Bibi looked at me.

'Well?'

'She seems a nice girl.'

'Reliable?'

'Yes, reliable.'

'Good. I'll tell Sister Aloysius. I think she's a little unsettled at the moment . . . but reliable. Sister says she's very reliable. Do eat your brack.'

'Yes.'

'Goodbye then.'

She dropped a kiss on the top of my head.

'I'll see you tomorrow. Don't overdo things. You're looking terrible . . . tired, I mean. Very tired.'

'I feel fine.'

'I'll see you tomorrow.'

I waved at her.

She closed the door and I listened till I heard their feet cross the hall and the hall door close and then I threw up her bloody brack and her tea into the fireplace. Oh God.

* * *

The house smelled of cats, lazy urban cats that slept all day on the hall table among the piles of apparently forgotten letters, or on the armchair half way between the telephone and the door on the return landing that led to Constance's bathroom . . . a room that had once been a sturdy if not beautiful Victorian conservatory. Slatted shelves for holding pots of plants still ran round the brick base. From waist height up, most of the glass panes had been painted white, in the interests of privacy. Here and there a few unpainted panes let in the light and, when opened with difficulty, let out the steam. A glass door led out on to some iron steps which curled down into a small garden with a chestnut tree at one end which most effectively protected the house from any sun that might be around. The cats were very partial to the bathroom and at least one was always to be found asleep on the shelf, or on the little wicker chair beside the bath, or even in the bath itself. They seemed to grow there, Constance thought, as the palms and aspidistras had done so long before. Two rooms, each with its own high window looking out over the chestnut tree, had been made out of one bigger room and the kitchen stuck out on metal stilts over what had once been a small yard.

'Allow, lav,' said the milkman as he passed her on the stairs, carrying his orange crate of bottles and half bottles.

'Hello.'

She put the money in neat piles, shillings, sixpences and pennies on top of the telephone coin box. A cat rubbed its head around her ankles for a moment and then disappeared into the darkness of the passage. The milkman whistled on the second floor. She dialled the exchange. Father always said that milkmen were the great crooks of the world. Sid, this one was called. He didn't look like a crook, just pleased like everyone else that you came across that there was peace, not war.

'Hallo.'

'Bibi. Hallo.' She rattled coins into the box.

'Hallo?'

'Bibi. It's me. Hallo.'

'Where are you? You sound terribly close.'

'In my flat. I have a flat.'

'Super.'

A certain uninterest.

'It's great. Two rooms. It was all terrific luck. A real flat. I don't have to share anything with anyone.'

'Where is it?'

'Notting Hill.'

'Is it near Harrods?'

Bibi only knew the best places.

'Not too far. Tell Mother, will you? Tell her I've got a flat. All mod cons. You can come over and stay.'

'Super.'

'Better still a job . . . so she doesn't have to worry about me. No one has to worry.'

'I don't think anyone was. You know Mother only worries about what is directly under her nose and Father doesn't worry at all. What's the job anyway?'

'It's no great shakes at the moment, but it's money. I'm sort of sweeping the floor in an advertising agency, making the tea, odd jobs. Menial but with prospects.'

'Guinness is Good for You? That sort of thing?'

'That sort of thing.'

'That shouldn't tire your mind too much.'

Pip pip pip.

Constance pushed some more money into the slot.

'And you . . . how are you?'

'Marvellous. You're missing a lot of super parties. I suppose there are lots over there.'

'Not really. How's Charles? Is he still around?'

'He's doing his bar finals next week. He's working hard. There's no need I say . . . he'll sail through.'

'Of course.'

'That's what I tell him. Bill is going out with Angela Dillon.'

'Poor Bill.'

'He seems to be enjoying it.'

Burnt boats.

'Though I daresay . . .'

'What?'

'Oh nothing. Nothing.'

'Mother and Father?'

'Well. The same. Mother's frantically busy. Father's away at the moment. Nothing changes.'

'Good. That's what you want to hear when you are away.'

'Oh, Constance . . .'

'Yes?'

She thought the better of what she wanted to say.

'It doesn't matter. This must be costing you a lot of money. There's no news here. It just goes on. I'll tell them you're well. I'll tell them about Guinness is Good for You.'

'Yes. Thank you. Do come over and stay. There's a bed you know. Always.'

'Mmmm.'

Pip pip pip.

'Goodbye. Bibi. Goodbye.'

Silence.

Sid the milkman rattling on the stairs.

'Tra then, lav. Tra.'

'Tra.'

*   *   *

After about half an hour's writing my hand gets tired. My fingers ache with the effort of gripping the pen. I can't use the typewriter at all. The pressure of my fingers on the keys creates avenues of pain up through my arms and into the back of my head. Maybe that girl, whatshername, will have sense, will be able to get the words, full stops and commas down on to the paper for me. How angry Bibi will be when she finds the house still sty-like, the dishes unwashed, dust gathering and the two of us absorbed in my probably pointless effort to create. My eleventh hour comment on myself . . . a non-Odyssey if ever there was one. I am experiencing a speeding up of the ageing process, rushing through in six months the withering that normally takes fifteen or even twenty years. I am learning, but without time for adjustment, of the creeping incapacities of the body, the curious centralising of the mind on the past, the gradual withdrawal of yourself from the main current of the living, the pleasurable or distasteful contacts with other people, living people. I dwindle in front of my own eyes, unlike the normally ageing who only diminish in the eyes of others.

I would like to go to St Mary's church on Christmas day, not, I am afraid, for spiritual reasons, but to fill my nose again with the smell of the dusty hassocks and the brass polish, feel the barely warm air stirring lazily up through the metal grills in the aisle, be safe for a moment in the knowledge that nothing has changed. The plaster crumbles from the walls; the words remain. The unpruned branches of the plane tree scrape against the high windows. The words are there on the tissue pages. Now Lord, lettest Thou Thy servant depart in peace according to Thy word . . . No. Christmas is jubilation.

We, Bibi and I, were sent ahead to walk with Nanny. Socks pulled tight up to the knees and held with black elastic garters that left a pattern on your legs that never faded through the winter months. Hats tied firmly under the chin with velvet ribbons that matched the collars of our coats. Two pennies for the collection tucked down safely into the palm of one of the fur-lined leather gloves. For mine eyes have seen Thy salvation, which Thou hast prepared before the face of all the people. The rector's voice tumbled from peeling wall to peeling wall as he prayed for the soldiers and sailors fighting in the war, and the sick and needy of the parish and the governments of the sick world and send them wisdom and peace be with you . . . and with Thy spirit. I never really gave it all a second thought and Bibi turned to Charles and Rome with an enthusiasm that turned as the years went by to an almost evangelical sternness; gaiety and happiness were replaced by duty and virtue.

*   *   *

'Why do you sit there in the dark, Constance? It is Constance, isn't it?'

Mother spoke peevishly from the doorway.

'Yes. I am Constance.'

'I seem to have mislaid my glasses. I really don't see things as well as I should without my glasses. Tiresome. I had such excellent sight. You just seem to sit around all the time doing nothing. You used to do that as a child, too. Mooning. Staring into space. Wasting time.'

'I'm thinking, Mother.'

'That's what you always used to say, if I remember correctly. That sort of behaviour never gets one anywhere. Did it get you anywhere?'

'No, Mother. I don't suppose it did.'

'I would have been surprised if you had made anything of your life. I knew when you left Trinity like that that you had no . . . staying power. That chimney needs cleaning.'

A small twist of smoke had escaped into the room. She coughed discreetly, holding the back of her hand against her pursed lips.

'Neither of us made too much of ourselves really, did we?'

'Bibi is married. She has four lovely children. She has a place. While . . .'

'I always used to wonder why you married Father.' I interrupted her before she could finish.

'I always suspected you were thinking impertinent thoughts.' There was a ghost of a smile on her face.

'You never seemed to me to be compatible. Maybe I was wrong.'

'He gave me everything I wanted and left me alone. I would have thought it was a very good arrangement. He would have liked a son. We would both have . . . If only . . . It was as good a marriage as most, I would imagine.'

The wind rattled the unpruned creeper against the window. Mother shivered slightly and took a step towards the fire.

'It never used to be cold like this. The fire won't draw properly until you get that chimney cleaned. Mr Fannin . . .'

'Yes. I'll do that.'

'And remember to get out the dust sheets . . . the books . . .'

'It's all right. I remember.'

'He really preferred the company of men. A misogynist . . . is that the word? Misogynist. I don't mean that he . . .'

'Of course not.'

'There have always been a lot of men like that. They need women, but don't like them. Something to do, I suppose, with the way they were brought up. It never worried me.'

'Did it never enter your head that maybe he had a . . . well a lady somewhere? After all, those late nights at the club, all those weekends away. Didn't you ever . . . ?'

She shook her head abruptly.

'What a silly question. Barbara would never have asked such a silly question. Switch on the light. This darkness is very trying.'

I stretched out my hand and the bulb flowered on the table lamp. I was alone and the fire was in need of serious attention.

*   *   *

He was lying beside her, his hands laced behind his head staring up at the bright reflections from the sea that moved constantly on the ceiling.

'Good morning.'

He continued to stare as if hypnotised by the glimmering movement, but he smiled as he spoke.

'Was I all right?'

Then she blushed. Her entire body felt as if it were blushing.

'Oh God,' she said. 'I really do apologise, for saying a damnfool thing like that. It just slipped out. Consider it unsaid. I just wouldn't like to think . . .'

He turned over on his side and looked at her.

'Don't worry, Irish. You were okay. Next time you will be better. Practice is what makes perfect. You must learn to relex. That is important. Relex. It is not like driving a car.'

'I don't drive a car.'

'You know what I mean.'

'Yes.'

'You don't even relex when you are sleeping. Your hands are knotted into little fists. I watch.'

'I suppose I've always been like that. I'm a nervous type.'

'Men have in their heads such fantasies. Such dreams of . .'

'The perfect fuck?'

'I would not have put it quite like that.'

'So it never works out the way you want it to?'

'Not really. Perhaps more interesting ... perhaps ... oh I don't know. Sometimes our imaginations carry us beyond our sad bodies' capabilities.'

'You do it a lot?'

He laughed.

'No, Irish woman. From time to time. That's all. My imaginings keep me going, better most times than the reality.' He put out a hand and touched her bare shoulder gently. 'I like this reality though. I like your nervous face. I like you. Now, I will make some coffee and then I must work for two hours. I have each day to work for two hours. It is my rule. If I do not keep to my rule my life seems to crumble a little. You will go to the hotel and get your baggage and bring them here. Yes?'

He threw back the sheet and got out of bed. He stood in the sun stroking his stomach abstractedly. Unlike her father, he seemed unperturbed by the drooping flesh.

'Do you ... Are you sure?'

'I am sure. We won't set the world on fire. For a little while we will struggle to be a little content. That is a good therapy.'

He looked down at her and smiled. 'Look out of the window.'

She sat up and looked out of the window. Across the road a low wall separated them from the stony beach and the sea. Red and brown nets clothed the wall. The sea was bright with sun. The leaves on the oleanders barely moved. Two old men on wooden chairs bent over the nets, their figures twisting at the ropes, their heads nodding as they talked.

'It is such a landscape for relexing, you agree?'

'Yes.'

'After lunch we will swim. I have a very good place to swim. The sea there is green like I have seen nowhere else.'

'You do like things to be organised, don't you?'

He bent down and picked up his trousers from the floor.

'I am sorry. Always I make plens. Sometimes I forget that . . . too there are other people. It is for me important to know what I am doing every moment of the day. Every day of my life. I work, I read, I eat, I relex, sleep. Each time it is plenned. Plens are my safety.'

'No room for surprises?'

'No. If possible, no. What do I say? You are a surprise, Irish. But one surprise is enough for a very long time.'

She laughed.

'What a ridiculous man you are. Right ho . . . you make the plans and I'll do the cooking. How about that? If I don't like your plans, I'll tell you. If you don't like my cooking, you tell me.'

'Coffee,' he said, and dropped his trousers on the floor again. He went into the large cupboard that was the kitchen and she heard him strike a match and turn on the gas.

'While the kettle boils I will put myself in the shower and after you can do that too.'

'Yes, please. Sex makes you smell.'

He laughed.

'A good smell, Irish woman, don't you think?'

'I'll have to get used to it.'

He ran water into the kettle. As he turned on the tap there was a gentle knocking in the pipes, rhythmic and rather reassuring. She lay back into the pillows and closed her eyes.

'I bet you're an early rising freak. What time is it?'

His bare feet padded across the floor to the bathroom.

'Twenty-five minutes to eight.'

'Jacob. Oh Mamma mia.'

'Always I get up at half past seven. From many years I have done that. There is more space in the world in the early morning. Your thoughts can grow and then they must shrink again when people start to rub against them. If I was a really strong man I would get up at five, but I find that too hard. The body clock says no.'

'My body clock says no to twenty-five minutes to eight.'

'Rabbitch.'

He went into the bathroom.

Rabbitch, she thought, is a good word, I must incorporate it into my vocabulary. The pipes rattled again and the smell of steam floated into the room. Outside two scooters roared past and a man's voice called.

'Mario! È, Mario!'

There was no reply. Twenty-five to eight was also too early for Mario. I wonder if I have a child inside me. A small explosion of life. I suppose that's a bit too much to expect. They say as you get older it's less likely to happen. How aggravating it would be if my plan went wrong. However, it will have been a good dream, and unlike most dreams I will be able to remember it. Call it back at will.

'Mario!'

How strange to be listening to those rattlings and splashings for the first time. To have shared my body's privacy with a stranger. Am I now a different person? Whole, perhaps, for the first time? I don't believe that I am any different. A little more aware, perhaps, of my own vanity that won't allow me to vanish irrevocably from the world, leave no trace. I had hoped, foolishly I now see, to write myself into some form of immortality. Now I must rely on the more conventional seed. How angry Mother would be if she knew what I was up to. And Bibi, she would be displeased rather than angry. Stern displeasure is her weapon, her overt weapon, but she will also use her secret weapon; she will pray for me.

'Constance.'

She opened her eyes. He was standing beside her, dressed now, holding a cup of coffee towards her.

'You've been asleep again. That's a good sign.'

'Am I a monster, do you think?'

She sat up as she spoke and took the cup from him.

'Probably. But just a little monster.'

'How dreary to be just a little monster.'

'Drink your coffee. Your country breeds monsters. Since pre-history times. You are just conforming to the national pattern.'

'Ouch.'

'I make good coffee, yes?'

'Yes.'

'Mario!'

Shutters were rattled open and a torrent of incomprehensible words were thrown down into the street.

✻ ✻ ✻

I find it increasingly hard to keep a check on the passage of time. The winter darkness makes it almost impossible for me to tell instantly if it is morning or evening. My hunger clock no longer functions. How long is it since I last moved from this chair? Do I sleep at night or in the day time? Bibi was here. I remember that, but when? Was it an hour ago, or maybe yesterday? Unlike those men in prison who keep track of time by marking each passing day by a scratch on the wall, I seem no longer to have a need for such an acknowledgment. A long winter day surrounds me, which can only have one end. The fire has gone out. I must see to that. Scrape among the ashes, shovel away the cinders. First, I must find the whiskey. If only I could remember where I had put the bottle. It is so silly, all those yesterdays in the hollow of my hand, overflowing memories and I can't find the whiskey bottle now, now when I need it. My only need. Somewhere I lost God too, through carelessness, I think, rather than design. I was His child, undoubtedly, in the knee socks and garters. I believed then with conviction and gratitude in His system of punishment and reward, His just compassion, the glorious vision of joyful eternity. As I outgrew my conviction I neglected to replace it and one day God was gone and I was sad because it meant that I was no longer a child and glad because I knew that then I could make my own rules. Blue lights dazzling on the Christmas tree, that's what I need now. The bottle first, then, the blue lights. Then there will be gaiety again.

'The fire is out.'

Bill seemed so tall. He stood there between me and the door and filled the room.

'What day is it?'

'Wednesday.'

'Wednesday.' I repeated it to myself, embedding the information in my mind.

'What time?'

'About eleven.'

'Good God.'

He walked across the room and pulled back the curtains. It was grey, but definitely day time.

'I keep losing bits of time. I don't think I've been to bed.'

'You don't look as if you've been to bed.'

'I was just about to have a drink . . . a reviving drink. Have you time to have one with me . . . or inclination?'

He looked at me for a moment.

'A small one. Yes.'

'The major problem being . . . I've lost the bottle.'

'You look for the bottle, I'll deal with the fire. It's freezing in here. Have you an ash bucket and sticks and things like that?'

'You shouldn't . . .'

'You shouldn't argue with your doctor.'

With a great effort, I got out of the chair.

'By the kitchen door you'll find everything. Joe deals with all the ashes and things when he comes on Thursday. Would you really prefer coffee? Tell me the truth.'

'Yes. If that's not too much of a bother.'

'Coffee it shall be.'

'The slightest whiff of alcohol might alarm my patients. Models of sobriety and health they like their medical men to be.'

He followed me as I walked slowly across the hall. Left, right, left, right. I am the master of my feet. I could feel him watching me.

'Constance . . .'

'Just do the fire, Bill. Please.'

I turned on the tap and waited with a finger under it for the water to run hot, then I filled the bottom of the coffee pot.

'I make good coffee, Irish woman. In the whole world I make the best coffee.'

'Rabbitch,' I said, annoyed.

'What?' asked Bill.

'Oh . . . nothing. A goose walked over my grave.'

He left the room with the kindling and the ash bucket.

I put the black oily beans into the grinder and switched it on.

'A big jug and boiling water. None of these modern machines are necessary for the making of excellent coffee.'

'Leave me alone, you Polish bully.'

I whispered the words angrily, so that Bill wouldn't hear me speaking. Someone laughed. I tipped the coffee into the pot and screwed the top on and put it on the gas. I could hear Bill rattling and scraping in the next room. I hoped his patients didn't mind him smelling of ashes. Cups, sugar, spoons, milk. I opened the fridge door and Bibi's quiche caught my eye reproachfully. I took out the milk and slammed the door. The girl, whatsername will be coming. She can eat it. It will be her duty to eat it before Bibi arrives again.

'There we are.'

Bill put the bucket down by the back door.

'I'll just wash my hands. I'd have made a very good housemaid.'

'I bet you don't do the fires at home.'

'Of course not. What do you think I got married for? Nor do I clean my shoes, nor put away my clothes. I just leave them on the floor. Anyway we have central heating.'

'See what I was saved.'

'Perhaps with you it would have been different.'

'I shouldn't think so. We'd both have been disgruntled. An ageing disgruntled pair.'

'Like most other pairs.'

'Probably.'

'I'll take the tray. You carry the coffee pot.'

I turned off the gas and picked up the pot. A new, unopened bottle of whiskey stood on the shelf by the door. No more searching problems. Even the feel of it in my hand was comforting.

'Constance . . . that bed is still waiting for you, you know. I'd like you to think about it sensibly.'

The fire was burning nobly in the grate between us.

I shook my head.

'Bibi has found me a girl. She's coming today. A nice girl. An orphan who has been trained to do as she is told, and be thankful for small mercies.'

'If I know you, you'll untrain her as quickly as possible.'

'She can fetch and carry. Won't that do? All I need is someone to fetch and carry and listen to me if I feel like talking. Just be here . . . in case of emergencies. Don't bully me, Bill. This is the way I want it. Really it is.'

'It's all right, Constance. I give up. You don't have to worry.'

'Promise.'

'Promise.'

'How's Angela?'

'Rushed off her feet. You know, Christmas and all that ... in good form. Yes, good form. Thanks.'

'And the children?'

'Just like everyone else's I suppose. They sit around and blast themselves into unconsciousness with incredible sound. Really aggressive sound. It's impossible to hide from it. It seems to beat all the energy out of them. Christina is going to Trinity in the autumn.'

'That old? How it all rushes away and then starts all over again. What's she going to read?'

'Medicine. If she gets good enough results. There's no scraping in these days because someone knows your father. Sometimes, when I'm not hating them all, I feel rather sorry for the young. They don't have fun any longer ... when I look back at the fun we had ...'

'Every generation makes its own fun.'

'I suppose so.'

'They would despise our fun, if we were able to describe it for them.'

'You can't go to Brittas any more now. We went down for a day last summer, and I said never again. Millions of swarming people. Bungalows everywhere and caravans. It's hell. Like Sandymount strand on a Bank holiday.'

He stirred his coffee and thought about the ghastliness of it all.

'Angela never liked Brittas much anyway,' he said finally.

The whiskey in my cup had reached the pain, wrapped itself warmly round it, protected me for a moment, just for a moment.

'Do you know what I'd really like to have done?' he asked.

'What?'

'I always saw myself as a GP. Somewhere over in the West. Connemara, Galway, even Clare perhaps. Some small place where everyone knew everyone. And there was good fishing. An old house with a little bit of a farm on the side. I've always hated cities. Rat race is a good expression, whoever thought it up. An American, I suppose.'

'You could always up sticks and go.'

He laughed.

'I could in my eye.'

'Angela would object?'

'It's easy enough to blame other people for the mess you make of your own life.'

'Yes.'

'It's odd . . . I never wanted much, never had much ambition, you know . . . and I've got . . . well all anyone would want . . .'

'Two cars.'

He laughed.

'You've always cut me down to size.'

'I'm mean. We are all absurd . . . pathetic. Isn't it lucky I refused to marry you, otherwise you might now be a depressed doctor in Connemara, hurtling around those roads in an old car that let in the rain, hitting the bottle, perhaps secretly longing for the bright lights of Dublin, like membership of the RDS and consulting rooms in Fitzwilliam Square. Disgruntled. The peasants would love you because you'd forget to send them their bills, and the middle classes would talk to you agreeably in the golf club but take their illnesses to someone younger whose hands didn't shake.'

'You make me feel so good.'

'Have some more coffee.'

'A drop. Then I must get back on the road. My car doesn't let in the rain, it has a heater and a radio. I might even get round to putting in a sauna one day.'

'I'll have some more as well.'

I held out my cup towards him. He sat and stared at me for a long time before he moved to get the coffee, studying with his blue comfortable eyes the travesty of my body. I put my hand up in a gesture of protection.

'Oh, please don't.'

He stood up and touched my hand gently, then he splashed the remains of the coffee into both our cups.

'I like your company, Constance. I missed you all the years you were away. I imagine I will always miss you.'

'We used to dance well together.'

'Yes.'

'My feet don't work any longer. I suppose you still dance?'

'From time to time. I no longer get the same pleasure from it though.'

'What do you get pleasure from now?'

'Well . . . I don't know . . . it's no longer that explosive feeling I used to have from time to time when I . . . we . . . were young . . . oh, quite a few things really give me a feeling of passive well-being . . . racing in Dublin Bay on a fine Thursday evening, I don't even have to win, just be there; going for a really long walk in the mountains, alone, no people, no bloody chat; fishing; work, too, sometimes, the times when something out of the ordinary comes up, when I can really get the mind to work. A silly question. Not dancing anymore, that's for sure. I'll have to go, Constance. Most of my patients are suffering from pre-Christmas hysteria. I'll help you to your bed, friend. You look bloody. A sleep would do you all the good in the world. Tucked up and off your feet.'

'I can put myself to bed, thank you.'

'Don't argue with me, for heaven's sake.'

He meant it. I got up and walked towards my bedroom slowly. I had been stupid enough to leave the bottle behind on the table. He stood in front of the fireplace and watched me go. I was glad he didn't come with me as I still had enough vanity left in me not to want anyone, even my doctor, to see the ugly ruin of my body. I unpinned my skirt and pulled my jumper off. I sat down on the bed and pulled at my tights. My fingers throbbed with the effort. There was a ladder in one leg, spreading into an unexpected hole just below the knee. I heard his steps cross the hall.

'A moment,' I called. 'Just a moment.'

I lay back into the pillows and pulled the clothes around me.

'It's okay.'

He came in and walked across the room. He held the bottle in one hand.

'You forgot your life support.'

'Thank you.'

'Are you all right?'

'What a silly question to ask.'

'You know what I mean. Do you want a couple of pills before I go?'

'No. I have them there if I need them.'

'I'll be back. Take things easy, Constance.'

His head made a little swooping movement towards me as if he were going to kiss me, but then thought the better of it. He smiled.

'Goodbye.'

'Tara for now.'

He didn't turn at the door and wave or anything like that, just pulled it gently shut and went away.

*   *   *

The doctor wore a black coat and narrow striped trousers. The right side of his glasses slipped slightly sideways down towards a small mole on his cheek that sprouted neat hair. His hands were folded above the surface of his desk, as if in prayer. He waited until

Constance was seated firmly in her chair before he spoke.

'Well, Mrs ah . . .'

'Miss Keating,' she corrected.

He looked down briefly at the papers in front of him.

'Miss Keating,' he agreed.

Behind his left shoulder a pigeon sat on the window-sill pecking with enthusiasm among its feathers.

'Yes. Um. Yes. You are pregnant. That is correct. Twelve weeks, I should say.'

He didn't look very enthusiastic.

'How marvellous. How absolutely marvellous.'

He still didn't look very happy. A second pigeon joined its friend.

'Have you . . . ah . . . plans? Ah . . . marriage plans?'

'No. Definitely not. No marriage plans. It's all fine. It's what I wanted. Everything is working out just the way I wanted it to be. This is all just fine.'

'I see.'

The second pigeon nudged up closely to the first one. It looked to Constance like a take-over bid.

'Well, in that case,' he said, his hands becoming business-like, one of them reaching for his pen, the other straightening the papers on the desk in front of him, 'I suppose we should get down to brass tacks.'

'Yes, please. I do assure you, I am terribly pleased.'

He suddenly smiled at her.

'I'm glad,' he said. 'I'm happy for you. Now then . . .'

With a slight movement of its body the second pigeon nudged the first one over the edge of the sill and then calmly began to search among its own feathers for whatever it was that pigeons always seemed to search.

*　*　*

Someone was moving in the distance. A door banged, footsteps, then objects rattled, were picked up and heavily put down again. My eyes were too heavy to open so I lay there and listened. It couldn't be Mother. She had never rattled things or made clumsy gestures. She had moved smoothly through life until the end, when they had made her suffer in a way that she neither understood nor deserved. She had been a woman who had led a life very remote from anguish and then had had three months of it forced upon her by the people who were nearest to her. Some Divine test of spiritual stamina? Poor Mother. It was your only test in all those years, a wicked surprise for someone to spring on you. Steps across the hall. Bibi? No. She wouldn't be able to resist the temptation to come in and interfere with me in some way. Music murmured gently. I opened my eyes and looked at the ceiling. It wasn't much to look at. I had just decided to get up and go and investigate when the door opened and a girl's head poked into the room.

'Who's that?' I asked.

'It's me. Bridie. I looked in before but you were dead to the world. I hope I didn't wake you with the noise I've been making.'

'What time is it? I presume it's still Wednesday.'

'Half four.'

'Goodness, I really have slept. Come in. Let me have a look at you.'

'I've just wet the tea. Would you like a cup?'

'That would be very nice, thank you.'

The head disappeared.

Bridie what, I wondered. I punched a bit at my pillows and pulled myself up against them. The whiskey I had drunk in the morning soured the back of my mouth. Poor Bridie orphan, out of the frying pan into the fire. But then she could go. The minute she had the fare scraped together she could walk out of here and take the boat. Third class . . . no, no, they called it second class now. Progress.

'Do you want anything to eat?'

She pushed the door open with a foot and came into the room, a cup of tea steaming in each hand.

'No.'

She put one cup down on the table by the whiskey bottle and then sat down in the only chair that wasn't covered with mess. She stirred the tea and didn't speak a word.

'Have you been here long?'

'Mrs Barry left me round just after twelve. She said she'd try and get back this evening to see how you are. I tidied up the little room beyond the kitchen for myself. I hope that was the right thing to do.'

It had been a maid's bedroom in the past, very small and rather dark if I remembered right.

'That's not a very nice room.'

'It's okay. I've never slept in a room on my own before. I might get lost if it was too big. I think it's great.'

She sounded as if she meant it.

'Mrs Barry found me sheets and blankets and things. I have it all decorated.'

'Decorated?'

'Decorations. Chains and things. I got them in Woolies when I went for your lights.'

'Oh, yes. That's lovely.'

'I done the tree for you too. It looks gorgeous now. Just one mass of little blue lights. You owe me one pound twenty. I hope that's okay?'

'You've been very busy.'

'They taught me to work hard. Where's the point in sitting about?'

'What's your surname?'

She didn't answer.

'You know . . . the name that comes after Bridie?'

She thought for a long time before speaking.

'I was found on a seat in Herbert Park,' she said. 'Someone just left me on a seat. I often do go into the park and wonder to myself which seat was it. I think it would have been near the pond . . . where someone would find me before . . . I was well wrapped up. So they told me. I don't think anyone wanted me to die. I think it would have been near the pond. Wouldn't you think that?'

'Most probably.'

'It was May. It wasn't cold.'

'No. It wouldn't have been cold.'

'So they called me May. Bridie May. That's my name, I suppose.'

'It's a nice name. Bridie May. It sounds good.'

She smiled at me.

'I think so too.'

There was a long silence while we both sipped at our tea. They'd taught her to make a good cup of tea too, I thought.

'Do you have a washing machine?'

'No.'

'Oh.'

'Most of the stuff got moved out of the house after my father died. We were going to sell it, but then . . . well . . . it seemed expedient for me to come here.'

'There's an awful lot of dirty stuff around the place.'

'Yes. I'm sorry. I haven't felt up to . . .'

'That's all right.' she said abruptly. 'There's a launderette in Ballsbridge. I'll tie all the stuff up in a bundle and run down there before it closes. It'd be well to get it all out of the place quickly. Have you money?'

'In that drawer.'

I pointed to the chest of drawers.

'And take for the lights too, and the decorations in your room.'

She got up and went across the room. She opened the drawer and stood looking down into it.

'Do you just leave that money lying in there all the time?'

'Yes. It seems the easiest thing to do.'

'Loose. You shouldn't do that you know. There's people around . . . might take it.'

'I hope not. You take what you need.'

She took out four pound notes and held them up for me to see.

'That's four pound I'm taking. I'll put back the change later.'

'I'll get up and make myself sort of respectable while you're out.'

'Wouldn't you do well to stay where you are? Just for today. You look washed out.'

'I'll get up. I feel more like a human being when I'm up.'

She nodded and smiled. She was going to have trouble with her teeth if she didn't get out of the country soon. Two sets of china choppers, like so many others, before the age of twenty-five. A great deterrent to sin of course, if you looked at it sensibly. I waved my hand towards her, a friendly, meaningless gesture. She smiled again.

'I won't be long.'

She pushed the money into her pocket and left the room, closing the door gently behind her. I wondered if her mother had left Herbert Park and taken the first boat from DunLaoghaire. Had she stood on the deck looking at the receding city, the spires, the marshalled rows of houses, the dim hills, praying that someone would find the well-wrapped baby on the seat near the pond? In May it would have been a lovely evening, boats in the bay, and seagulls looping in the sky above the floating city. Maybe she didn't care, was just filled with an immense relief to be away from the pain, to be safe. We had walked and played in that park in the afternoons. Played grandmothers footsteps on the high stone steps at the end of the pond and fed the ducks with stale bread from a brown paper bag. Skipped, the warm smooth handles and the turning tapping rope, the panting breath and the murmuring voices ... Teddy bear, Teddy bear turn around, Teddy bear, Teddy bear touch the ground. Nanny and her friends strolled and sat and chatted, pushing and rocking the huge, polished prams. Knitting in the summer, under the shade of the long rose pergola, fingers flying, heads nodding, eyes always watching. Sometimes the glory of a band in the circular bandstand, the men in their navy uniforms, their instruments shining gold and silver in the sun. After each piece the conductor would bow carefully, his baton held out in front of him between two white gloved hands. We would clap. No one ever gave a thought to well-wrapped up ... up. Up. I must get up. Otherwise another day will be gone and I will have made no effort to live any part of it.

I smell of death these days. No matter how often I lather the soap on my body and wipe it away, no matter what I rub into my flaking skin, there is only temporary relief from the smell. It creeps out through my pores again and clings to my clothes contaminating anything I touch. It depresses me almost more than the pain. The blue lights on the tree are beautiful. Tiny, brilliant bulbs threaded through the green branches. She, whatsername, had left them switched on, so the moment I opened the door, they dazzled my eyes.

*　*　*

Lights were laced through the branches of the trees in the Piazza. The air was warm, below us in the bay the fishermen shone their spotlights into the sea.

'It's so bloody romantic,' said Constance.

He put his wine glass down on the table and gestured with one crippled hand towards the town below them curving along the edge of the sea. The lights, the oleanders, the coloured boats drawn up on the narrow beach, movements through the light and shadow, uncertain drifting sounds blown towards them by the velvet breeze.

'Don't be fooled by the pretty picture. The human savage is at work, even here, just the same as anywhere else in the world. The destroyers are always at work.'

'You don't like people much.'

'I don't say that. But I don't think we're poor courageous creatures, struggling against the odds towards some sort of magic perfection. I have not that romantic view of the world.'

He put his hands on the table in front of him and stared at them. Constance had noticed him doing this before as he searched in his mind for words.

She also stared for a moment at his hands and then blushed and looked away towards the sea and the romantic fishermen shining their lights.

'Things are better now,' she said, after a long silence. 'Better than they used to be. After all . . .'

'I tell you something, Irish woman.' He picked up his glass and took a long drink. He held the cool glass against his cheek as he spoke.

'I tell you things are worse. Now they try to destroy the soul of man, because it is not . . . expedient that man should have something as confusing, as tiresome as a soul. How can you fit a human soul into a computer? You smile. You think I joke. Truly I joke not. What the Nazis did to my people was nothing to what is slowly starting to happen now . . . the neutralisation of the spirit. Slow, painful, necessary total subjection. No more trabbles. No more questions. No more dreams.'

'Rabbitch,' she said. 'A load of Eastern European rabbitch.'

'I watched for day after day, year after year while my family, friends, enemies, my people went, walked through those doors. Simple people, complicated people, poor, rich, shoemakers, painters, musicians, farmers, bakers, writers, bums, holy men, shopkeepers, men of faith and cynics they all walked through those doors, or died as they stood beside you in the stinking lavatories. A whole race, a whole culture, tradition. It took so little time to destroy so much. One day I found I couldn't cry any more and then I knew that I also was destroyed, just as if I had gone through those doors with the rest.'

The lights from the trees were reflected in his eyes, like dying embers in a black fire.

'I talk too much.'

He took another drink and put the glass down on the table. A waiter moved past, looking curiously in their direction.

'When people can no longer cry then there is no more hope for humanity.'

'Don't you believe in anything?'

'Yes. Death. I believe in Death. Someone said it is the crown of life.'

He laughed.

'I am very drank maybe. Perhaps you are right I speak rabbitch. Mournful rabbitch. Listen, Irish, when I die there will be no more of Isaac and Joseph and Ezriel or of Joel, my father. I am the last seed. No one will remember, pray for, Zelda my mother. No one will remember her red hair. No one will speak their names again. In the whole eternity of living there will be no one to care.'

'But perhaps . . .' her voice was tentative '. . . in a hundred years' time someone . . . somewhere someone may read one of your books and say then . . . say once there was this Jewish, Polish, British man called Jacob Weinberg and today he has become a part of me. Today I am different . . . extended. I mean . . . that does happen, that has to happen.'

He laughed again, this time with a curious joy.

'You are not a lady it is easy to make mournful.'

'No. I hate to lose my equilibrium. I look after myself very well. I think that's why I can't write with any success. I have the right instincts, but I have no courage. It's like I can't dive. I can climb into the sea, walk in, even jump in if I have to, but put my head down and dive . . . oh no. I even get nightmares about it sometimes.'

He put his hand on hers.

'I think I am a very boring person,' she said.

'I am not bored.'

'No. Not yet. There won't be time for that. Should we have another drink?'

'Of course. But at home.'

'Yes. Home.'

*   *   *

If I could pray . . . no, what I really mean is, if I had any conviction that my prayers might be listened to with attention, let alone answered . . . I would pray that in the next few weeks or days or whatever may be ahead of me, that I may be able to see accurately with my mind, see the pattern. There has to be a pattern. I would pray if I could to find it, in the silence of my heart. All these years I have mistreated my mind, as I have mistreated my body; both are the victims of my carelessness, my sloth and my innate conviction that tomorrow would be time enough for attack, courage, commitment. Now, I have only the energy left to laugh. I am stuck with my own laughter. The rug in front of the fire is freckled with burns, pale brown, like the tiny moles scattered across the skin of old people; on the backs of their hands, their wrists, their shoulders, perhaps even on more private skin. I will be spared that, and the possible problems of false teeth, incontinence and senility. Comfort, great comfort that.

'What on earth are you doing standing there like a zombie?'

Bibi's firm hand pushed me down into a chair.

'Sometimes I think you're going absolutely potty.'

She sat down opposite me.

'What a day I've had. The children all go in totally different directions. They all send their love, by the way. They're all dying to see you. They'll be over in the next day or two. Not all at once, of course, that would be completely exhausting. William has grown out of all his clothes. Shot up. He must be nearly as tall as Charles now. Out of everything. You'll hardly recognise him. The girl is making a cup of tea. I met her coming up the steps. I think she's going to be all right, don't you? You mustn't ruin her you know. You probably will. You've so little sense. However . . . How nice the tree is. Sweet, all those blue lights. If you give me a list of presents I'll get them for you . . . actually the girl could, couldn't she? I'm sure she'd love a little run into town.'

She stopped talking and looked at me, one of her small white teeth gnawing nervously at her bottom lip.

'How are you feeling?'

'Not too bad. I spent the morning in bed.'

'How sensible of you.'

'Not really. I wouldn't have done it if Bill hadn't ordered me to.'

'I don't know what we'd do without Bill.'

'Three cheers for Bill.'

'Constance . . . please take that bed in the hospital. Please.'

'I've said no. I mean no. For heaven's sake, Bibi, remember what you did to Mother. You can't in all conscience want to do that to me too.'

'You're totally unaware of what can be done nowa—'

'I am totally aware of what can't be done, dear sister. No one can re-create me. No one. I'm going to die, and as far as I'm concerned I have the right to say at least where I want to die, if nothing else.'

'It's most unfair of you to throw poor Mother's illness in my face.

Everything that could be done for her, was done. You know that perfectly well. No expense was spared. No stone, not one stone left unturned. You know . . . you know . . . everything. You came over and saw.'

'I saw an old woman who should have been dead being kept alive and tormented by the whole process just to make you and all the doctors and nurses feel good.'

'That is most unfair. You don't know what you're talking about. You're sick in your mind. You've always been a selfish, irresponsible brat. We had to decide. You just sat over there in London, with your touch-me-not airs. You got on with your own life, whatever that was, and had the nerve to abuse me down the telephone. That's easy to do, let other people make the decisions and then abuse them for it. Father was no help, but at least he kept out of the way. I'll write the cheques, he said, and went off to the country. I'll pay, pay anything, just see that your mother's treated well. I was alone. I had to make the . . . I had to take all the responsibility. I believe we did the right thing. You can't just let someone die. You must not, you really must not.'

'Don't be so damn stupid, Bibi, if she'd been some poor old woman with no money everyone'd have let her die quick enough. No discussions, no decisions. If no one had been able to afford to buy her three months of hell.'

'How can you say such terrible things to me?'

'I'm sorry, Bibi. Truly I am. It's just a bit near the bone. I just want to see it through in my own way. Have that little bit of freedom. I really don't want to hurt you. But I suppose I will, if I have to. I'm sorry. We've never been on the same side, have we?'

'Human life is a sacred gift . . .'

'Yes, sister, dear sister . . .'

The door opened and Bridie came into the room with a tray.

Bibi closed her angry mouth into a thin line and stared at the fireplace.

'Tea . . . ah. Thank you, Bridie. Put it here, would you?' I patted the table beside me with my hand. Mother's teapot and the sugar bowl and even the spoons had been polished and someone had removed the brown stains from the insides of the teacups with Vim. It all looked very old-fashioned, very *comme il faut*. Bibi still stared at the fireplace.

'That looks lovely. You've done a great job on the silver. Look, Bibi, Mother's pot, clean for the first time for years.'

'Mrs Barry brought the cake.'

A large squishy chocolate cake sat on a china plate.

'How lovely. Thank you Bibi.'

'Would there be anything else you would like?'

'No thanks, Bridie. That's the lot.'

She nodded, threw a quick look in Bibi's direction and left the room, closing the door discreetly behind her.

I poured a cup of tea and handed it to Bibi. She balanced it on the arm of her chair.

'Cake?'

'Every possible thing that could be done.'

'Cake?'

'You have no right whatsoever to criticise.'

'I know. Forgive me. Have a piece of cake. Here.'

I cut her a large piece and shovelled it on to a plate with the knife.

'Here. We mustn't quarrel. I only want to make it clear that I want to die in my own way. I don't want to have to be brave and grateful and helpless. I just want to die. Now, or tomorrow, or next week. Whenever it comes. I don't want to fight it.'

I held the plate out towards her. She took it from me and crumbled a little piece of cake between her fingers.

'We have a lot of genes and some memories in common. That's all. You don't have to make any decisions for me. I suppose you can pray for me if you want to. And mind the child.'

There was a very long silence. I cut myself a very small piece of cake and fiddled with it, so as not to upset her.

'You're so silly,' she said at last. 'You're not going to die. I don't know where you get this crazy idea. If you go into hospital, like any normal person would and get treatment, there is no reason why you should die. No reason . . . No reason . . .'

'I have written to the child's father.'

'You what?'

'Written. He will come. I'm sure he will, and listen to me, Bibi . . . there's to be no funny stuff when he comes. No hassle.'

'You really have gone out of your mind. Do you mean to say that some deadbeat foreign Jew is going to be allowed to come and take the child . . .'

'Hang on, hang on. Just a minute.'

She pushed a piece of cake into her mouth and glared at me as she chewed.

'What do you mean, deadbeat?'

'He's . . .'

'He's foreign. Right ho. I can't argue with that. Most people are after all foreign. He considers himself to be British, if that makes things any better. He's Jewish . . . that's right. He's got a big nose and broken hands, because a lot of nice clean-living Germans didn't like foreigners with big noses. But deadbeat, he's not. So what do you mean, deadbeat?'

'What do we know about him? You can't expect us to allow a man none of us know anything about to come and . . . and . . . Honestly, Constance.'

'I know about him. Won't that do? He's a most distinguished and successful writer.'

That startled her. She raised the teacup to her lips and eyed me carefully over it, trying to work out if I were lying or not.

'Really?' she asked cautiously.

'Really.'

'Would I have read any of his books?'

'I don't know. His name is Jacob Weinberg. I don't want to talk about him, but if he comes I want him to take the child. I want him to give her a name. That's what I want. Of course, he may not come.'

'Indeed he may not. I think I know that name. I don't think I've actually read anything of his, but the name rings a bell.'

She finished up the cake in silence, listening to the bells ringing in her head.

'I don't know what Charles will say.'

'There isn't much in the end of all that Charles can say.'

She wiped the remains of chocolate cake from round her lips with her handkerchief and then stood up.

'I have to fly. I didn't mean to stay more than a . . . goodness, look at the time! I have to collect Stella from the Jamesons. She'll kill me. I'll try and get some of . . . what did you say his name is?'

'Jacob Weinberg. W.e.i.n . . .'

'I know how to spell Weinberg. Some of his books. Hodges Figgis, perhaps.'

'They're probably banned here.'

'Banned . . .'

'Well . . . after . . . it's a sort of accolade really. You haven't reached the top if you're not banned in Ireland. I joke. I promise you I joke, Bibi. He's a real writer, a proper writer. I always have to make silly jokes.'

I shut my eyes and hoped that when I opened them she would be gone. She wasn't. She stood by the door fiddling with her handbag.

'Oh Bibi . . .'

She made me feel so guilty, so shameful somehow. The pain I was causing her would wipe off her face with cotton wool and cleanser when she had her evening bath, but I still felt guilty.

'. . . Just, thanks. I really mean that. Thanks for everything. Thanks a million.'

She smiled, a truly Christian, charitable smile. It was all I needed. I closed my eyes again. I heard the door open.

'I'll see you tomorrow. Maybe I'll bring the boys. If there's anything you need, just give me a ring.'

I heard the door close. I just sat there with my eyes closed. After a few minutes the door opened again, but it was only Bridie coming into the room.

'Are you all right?'

'Fine. Have a piece of cake.'

She put some wood on the fire and then crossed the room and pulled the curtains. I opened my eyes and watched her.

'I'll get even lazier with you around.'

'Where's the harm?'

'Have a piece of cake.'

'Yes.'

'And a cup of coldish tea.'

'I have some in the kitchen.'

'Go and get it and bring it in here . . . and bring me a glass of whiskey while you're at it.'

'Mrs Barry . . .'

'A large glass of whiskey with just a splash of water, please.'

A smile moved on the girl's face as she left the room.

The day of my mother's funeral, it had snowed. The rector's face was tight with cold as he spoke those words and the east wind pulled dangerously at his robes and rustled the pages of his prayer book. My father stood at the grave's edge, his face hidden by the brim of his black hat and the turned up collar of his coat. Bibi cried. 'He should take his hat off,' she sniffed into my ear at one moment, and I smiled. I covered my face with my handkerchief so that no one would see the smile. Wind and snow whipped at the words and muffled the sounds of the mourners' feet as they walked from the grave. Black ghosts, heads down against the wind, shoulders scattered with snow, moved between grey memorials to mortality, also snow scattered. It would be nice to be buried in the spring; daffodils and larks in the clear air. A sentimental thought.

'She'd slay me if she knew.'

She put the glass down beside me and cut herself a giant slice of cake.

'She made me promise not to let you drink.'

'It's all right, Bridie. Even the doctor says I may drink myself to death if I want to. Poor Bibi.'

She sat herself down in the chair that still must have held the warmth of Bibi's body.

'I'm free,' she said suddenly. 'That's why I took such a big piece of cake. I know I shouldn't. It was greedy, bad-mannered, all that sort of thing. But I did it just the same.' She burst out laughing.

'I'll have to eat it all now, even if it makes me sick, won't I?'

'You could always throw it in the fire.'

She shook her head.

'I'm too greedy. The only thing that will ever stop me from stuffing myself all day with gorgeous food is that I don't want to be fifteen stone. I could get like that, I think. I see my mother as a very fat woman. Someone you could cut slices off and she'd never notice.'

'Poor lady.'

'Maybe she likes it. There are lots of people who do. There was this very fat nun in the home. She was nice. She always had a bar of chocolate in her pocket. She'd take it out and have a bite when she thought no one was looking. It always made me feel good when I caught her at it. I never let on I knew. Her insides must have been destroyed with chocolate.'

'Were they nice to you?'

She chewed at her cake for a long time.

'I wouldn't like to say anything against them. They weren't unkind. I have to say that. They weren't unkind. Oh God, it's great to be out.'

She wiped at her mouth with the back of her hand.

'You know, I think they thought I'd stay.'

'Stay?'

'Well . . . I was very keen once. When I was about thirteen. Never off my knees. I thought about it a lot. I might have gone for to be a nun . . . only . . .'

I watched her face. Even at this sunless time of year, freckles patterned the bridge of her nose and the pale young skin below her eyes. I felt momentarily sad for the mother who had never known the landscape of that face.

'. . . only I thought it mightn't be the right thing for me. I thought maybe I was only doing it because I didn't have a mother. I thought . . . well, I don't think I was good enough, like.'

'I'm sure you were good enough.'

'I couldn't ever stop asking questions. Every answer led to another question, if you know what I mean? I felt I couldn't ever be satisfied. I prayed God to stop making me ask questions.'

She looked across at me with a nervous little smile.

'But he didn't.'

'He's a sensible old gentleman.'

'Sensible?'

'Certainly. It really wouldn't have been right for a young girl who has never known anything of life at all. Not even . . . to shut herself up forever, make promises. Commit herself to something she couldn't possibly understand. A rotten mistake.'

'There's others do it. Two of the girls . . .'

'Maybe, but that doesn't make it right. And maybe God doesn't want them to do it, but they haven't bothered to find out.'

'One of the sisters said God would turn his face from me.'

'An unkind lie. The one great thing to remember about the old gentleman is that He turns his face from no one. Absolutely no one. If you believe in Him at all, you have to believe that. Get me another drink, there's a good girl.'

I held my empty glass towards her.

'I have this bloody pain.'

She stood up and took the glass from me.

'Pills? Medicine? Anything like that?'

'Just whiskey.'

She nodded and left the room.

* * *

She always wondered who read her work, the three novels that she had sent hopefully to various publishers. What sort of people were they who took home piles of typescript in the evening and spent a few hours flipping through the pages, letting their eyes stroll through the lines of black words? Hundreds and thousands of useless, wasted words. Someone's dead dreams in the pile on the right; distinct possibilities on the left.

The man had his back to the window as she came in the door, so she was only aware of his height and the paleness and blueness of his suit and the blackness of his hair as she walked the length of the room towards him. He stood there silently, unaccommodating, his hands hanging by his sides, the sunlight shifting through the green leaves on the trees outside the window.

'Sit down.'

She sat on the edge of an elegant chair and looked past him out into the shining garden. After a moment he sat too and turned so that she could at last see his face. He looked fatigued. It must be hell, she thought, at the top. There was so much silence around that she could hear the birds in the garden chirping; if the window had been open she could have heard the grass growing. She pinched the back of her left hand between the nails of her thumb and first finger, just stop, she warned herself, bloody stop. He stretched out a hand and pushed a cigarette box towards her. The silk cuff that covered his wrist was a marginally paler blue than the blue of his suit. If a miracle could translate me back to Notting Hill again, now, this here moment, now, I might promise never to write another word.

'Umm. No, thanks,' she said, referring to the cigarettes.

He withdrew his hand from the box and let it fall on to the red plastic cover of her typescript that lay in front of him on the desk.

'Why do you write?'

His voice was uninterested.

She opened the catch of her handbag and then closed it again.

He tapped the red cover impatiently as he waited for her answer.

'I . . . well . . . want to write. That's all I really want to do . . . write.'

'But why? Surely you must have some idea why?'

'Isn't it enough just to want to do something . . . itch to do it?'

'Have you anything to say?'

'I don't know.'

He looked displeased.

'I mean . . . I'll have to find that out as I go along.'

He flipped through the pages in front of him with a finger.

'I like to see the possibles,' he said. 'I like to judge for myself. You can tell. I,' he amended, 'can tell.'

He picked up the typescript and looked at it for a moment before offering it to her across the desk.

'You have a small talent. Quite an original eye. To be quite blunt Miss . . . ah . . . Keating is it? . . . Keating . . . there is no point in us publishing a marginal first novel if we don't feel strongly that a second novel will come along, and a third. Growth and development. No point at all. We are not a charitable organisation. No.' He allowed himself a slight smile at the thought. 'You have, as I said, a small talent, but I really don't see you developing. In fact, I would be very surprised if you ever wrote anything else.'

She took the papers from him and stood up. Her hands were shaking.

'Thank you,' she said. Her voice sounded thick and ugly. She turned away from the green shining window and walked towards the door. When she reached it, she turned round. He was rubbing fretfully at the hand that had held the red plastic folder, with a pale blue silk handkerchief.

'Goodbye,' she said.

He bowed towards her. No point in wasting more words than were absolutely necessary.

The sun was shining benignly in the windows of the tall houses, little eddies of city dust moved on the pavement. She stood for a moment on the steps outside the door and watched the cars go by. About twenty paces down the street to her right a litter basket hung on a lamp post. She walked quickly towards it, the red file in her hand. She shoved it right down amongst the old copies of the *Evening Standard*, the cigarette packets and the paper bags. Maybe, she thought, the man who emptied the bins might take it home and read it, and love it and feel his life was changed for having read it, on the other hand he might not.

'Bloody fucking bastard,' she said inelegantly and walked on.

* * *

Constance was lying in the bath in the steam filled conservatory when she heard Fred from the basement flat calling her name. It was a cold autumn evening and damp leaves from the trees in the next garden had gathered in small piles on the glass roof above her. They stirred in the wind, and sometimes tumbled across the slope like small playing animals.

'Coming.'

She stood up, shedding water, and wrapped a towel round her warm pink body. It always seemed to happen, nicely warm and the dirt softened up enough to slither off with the soap and the phone would ring. A bath was never the same after an interruption of this nature.

'Coming,' she shouted again, just in case he hadn't heard her the first time. Sometime or other, when she was rich, she would get a telephone of her own, with a long cord so that she could carry it from room to room, like they did in American movies. Steam burst out on the landing as she opened the door and ran down the stairs.

'Thanks,' she called after Fred's back as he retired down to his basement.

'Constance.'

'Hello, Bibi. Hello.'

'You always take so long. It costs a fortune just waiting for you.'

'I was in the bath.'

'Tiens.'

Oh God, thought Constance, is she still at that?

'How's everyone? Mother, Father? Everyone?'

'Fine, great. And you?'

'Okay.'

There was a long expensive pause. Water trickled down her legs and made a little pool on the carpet.

'Can you hear me?'

'You haven't said anything for me to hear.'

'I thought perhaps . . . I . . . Charles and I have just got engaged. I thought you'd like to know.'

'Oh Bibi. How perfectly splendid. What should I say? I'm delighted. Are you happy? I do hope you're happy.'

'Of course I'm happy. Tellement heureuse.'

'Then I'm happy too. When are you going to be married? I hope it's not going to be a seven-year engagement or something like that.'

'Don't be silly. June. We thought that would be the nicest month.'

'Of course, June.' It had to be June trala. It had to be June . . .

'Will you be a bridesmaid?'

'Shouldn't you have a lot of sweet little children? They look so much nicer than ageing sisters.'

Wedding in June, tralala the moon . . .

'I'm having lots of sweet little children and you and Charles's brother Timmy will be best man. I'd like you to do it.'

'As long as you don't expect me to wear yellow.'

'Why can't you ever be serious?'

'I am, deathly serious. Remember that yellow . . . ?'

'Constance.'

'. . . dress I had once. I looked hideous in it. That was the night you met . . .'

'Constance, shut up.'

She shut up.

'It's moral support I need. You can choose your own colour dress . . . well, within reason. Moral support. The wedding's to be in Donnybrook Chapel.'

'Donnybrook . . . ? Oh . . . I'd forgotten about Charles. Poor old Canon Brooks will be terribly upset. You were always such a credit to him. It just goes to show . . .'

'Listen to me.'

The pool around her feet had become rather cold.

'I'm receiving instruction.'

She thought of Alice in the pool of tears.

'Receiving what?'

The penny dropped.

'Oh . . . Instruction. Are you serious?'

Poor, poor Canon Brooks.

'Of course I'm serious.'

'Are . . .'

'I know I'm doing the right thing. I've been thinking about it for a long time. I'm hoping to be received into the Church in January.'

'I can't really say anything. I don't know enough about it.'

'No.'

'I just hope you're doing it for the right reasons.'

'You were always snotty about me, weren't you? You . . .'

'That's not true, Bibi. We're sisters. That doesn't mean we have to think the same. I want you to be happy. I hope you are aware of that.'

'I am doing it for the right reasons. I believe.'

'The One, True and Only Church?'

'It's impossible to talk about it to people who don't understand. People who sneer.'

'What about Mother and Father?'

'Father says nothing. He's the same as ever. I don't believe he cares one way or the other. He's very polite and then goes away. Mother though . . . she's a bit upset . . . that's one reason why . . .'

'I'll be your bridesmaid . . .'

'Great. That's really great. Charles will be so pleased, too.'

'. . . even if you force me to wear yellow. I hope I don't disgrace you by blessing myself backwards or something.'

'Tu es folle. Vraiment folle. You've made me very happy. I can cope with the aunts and all once I . . .'

'Goodbye, sister. Good luck.'

'Goodbye.'

The bathwater was cold by the time she got back to it and the leaves had scattered themselves into dreary dark patches that would rot and stick to the glass and eventually become a boring domestic problem.

* * *

Suppose I had married Bill and we had gone to Connemara and had six children, would we have been better people? Happier? Would I have comprehended more in that isolation than I succeeded in doing in the isolation I created for myself? Would I have been able to write, in those circumstances, the books that I wanted so much to write? Damn fool questions with no answers. My face was very warm, too warm, maybe I was running a low fever.

'Bridie, I think I'll have another drink.'

'Surely.'

To my surprise her voice answered me from the other side of the fireplace. I opened my eyes and saw her curled into my father's chair as if she had grown there. She got up and took my glass from the table.

'I didn't realise you were there.'

'I've been here for ages. Watching you. I got a little frightened. You look so small. You only notice how small people are when they are asleep. Perhaps you should go to bed. You look worn out.'

'Yes. When I've had my drink.'

She nodded. She had already brought the whiskey bottle and a jug of water in from the kitchen and put them on the table by the tree.

'Have you ever been to Connemara?'

What a stupid question.

'No.'

She smiled.

'I've not been anywhere much. Some people took us for a holiday to Wexford once. A few of us. We stayed in their home, just at the back of this big long beach. It was very kind of them. We were there for a week. They had no children of their own, so it was a real kindness. The sand was lovely, but it stuck to you, got in your clothes and your hair, all over your feet and in between your toes, rubbing off the skin. We had to be careful because she didn't like us trekking sand into her nice clean house, so she didn't. "Which of you girls is it has tracked the sand into my lounge?" she used to say. "Sand is to be kept out of doors." She'd get out the hoover and make us clean it all up. She wasn't bad though. It was kind of her to have us at all.'

'Do you swim?'

'Are you mad? What would I want to do that for? I wet me feet and that was enough for me. The water was freezing. The others went in. I watched them. I walked on the beach a lot. I like that. You could die in the sea. I'd rather die on land. In Grafton Street. I'd like to die in Grafton Street, looking into Brown Thomas's window at all the lovely things.'

I laughed.

'You have a long time ahead of you before that happens.'

'Sister Emmanuel says you have to be prepared for the miracle of death every single hour of every day. A state of perpetual readiness to meet God.'

'How gloomy of Sister Emmanuel.'

'No. Not really. She isn't gloomy. That's just her way of looking at things. She's nice. Remember, Bridie, you are a child of God. Her hands are always cold, like as if she's already dead. You can feel the coldness of them through your clothes when she touches you. My friend Josie says she must be anaemic. When you're anaemic, the blood doesn't get around your body fast enough to keep you warm.

Did you know that? She looks as if the blood doesn't reach her hands at all. They're white and cold and her nails have little ridges on them. She's nice. You'd like her. It doesn't matter that you have no father or mother on earth, just remember.'

She sat quite still in my father's chair and stared without seeing anything into the fire.

In the silence the bell from St Bartholomew's Church struck ten times. Another day wiped off the slate.

'Remember what?'

'Remember you are a child of God.' She whispered the words.

'It's as good a thing to remember as anything else.'

The firelight was reflected in her eyes. It was her first night of freedom.

'Are you very lonely?' I asked.

She smiled slightly.

'We always had to be in bed by ten. Teeth washed, no talking and clothes ready for the morning. I heard that bell ring a few minutes ago and I thought . . . here I am . . . and well . . . here I am.'

'If we're going to be here much longer we must put some coal on the fire. It's getting cold.'

'Yes. There'll be more snow. I think I should help you to bed.'

'I suppose that would be sensible. And what will you do?'

'I'll go to bed too . . . in a little while, when I feel like it.'

She got up from the chair and did a little dance towards the Christmas tree. She hummed an odd little made up tune to herself.

'When . . . I . . . ummumm feel like it. Then, then I'll go.'

The blue lights trembled as she moved.

✳   ✳   ✳

The first time that I experienced the reality of physical pain was when I was having the child. I had prepared myself both mentally and physically for the experience; I had read all the books, done all the exercises, learnt to relax, attended clinics and lectures and film shows. I had gone dutifully through the intelligent woman's guide to childbirth. Pain is a myth. We had absorbed the words as we lay on the floor practising our slow breathing and then our fast breathing. You may at moments experience slight discomfort, we were promised as we exercised our leg muscles; yet in the end of all, pain did exist. A vast pattern of pain, like some formal dance, advancing and retreating slow turns, advance, bow, return. Pause. Then the rhythm starting again beating in the pit of your body, advance, retreat, turn slowly, turn, pause. It didn't frighten me, even when the pauses became inadequate for me to collect my equilibrium. I am frightened now. There is no rhythm now. I get no warning. It is like being eaten by some animal that tears at me until its hunger is temporarily satisfied and then it sleeps uneasily until the hunger starts again. I stuff myself full of Bill's pills and wash them down with whiskey and then wait until my mind becomes so confused that I neither understand nor feel anything. At those moments my mother's face pushes itself before my eyes. Tiny hunted face, burnt out eyes, wisps of hair lank on her pillow. Not even a shadow of herself, rather some monstrous caricature.

'What have you done to her?'

The panic in my voice echoed off the pale green walls of the passage in the nursing home. A table outside her door was covered with flowers. The room itself had been filled with roses, carnations, irises, azaleas, but their smell was drowned by the smell of disease and fear.

'Why the hell don't you leave her alone?'

'Ssssh, Constance. You're upset. Of course you are. It's such ages since you've seen her. You're just catching her on a bad day. Tomorrow she may be as right as rain. Perky as anything, chatting away. She goes up and down. You must understand that.'

Her finger and thumb dug into my elbow, demanding restraint.

'We must never give up hope, give up trying. Doctor Butterworth says she is responding very well to treatment.'

My heels squeaked on the polished floor as I ran.

An elderly woman in a flowery overall was cleaning the brass in the church. She rattled knobs and handles with a yellow duster. The cold air was filled with the smell of Brasso. I walked up to the front pew, pulled out a hassock and knelt down. Last Sunday's flowers still drooped on the altar. I racked my brains to think of a prayer. They could do with some of her flowers around here, I thought. She had had a prie Dieu in her room, with tiny carved feet and an old tapestry kneeler. She used to pray every night before she went to bed. Our Father which art in heaven, Hallowed be Thy name.

I had found her at it once when I had not been able to sleep and had wandered into her room in search of possible company. She hadn't moved when I opened the door. Her head was bent over her clasped hands and the light from the lamp beside her bed shone in the long hair which was hanging round her shoulders, like a young girl's hair. I loved her at that secret moment. I slipped out of the room without speaking.

Thy Kingdom come; Thy will be done on earth as it is in heaven. Thy will be done. Let Thy will be to take her now. As I speak. The lady with the brass polish moved past me up to start work on the altar rail, and possibly keep an eye on me. I could see by her face that she thought home was the best place for prayer, except for the ordered hours on Sunday and Holy days.

Hear me. Mercifully hear me.

Of course I realise the irony that Bibi is at this moment probably in some church, saying Oh Lord please let her live. So where does that leave You, oh Lord?

I imagine she carries more clout than I do.

Nonetheless, I would be grateful, Lord, if You would let her depart in peace. Soon. Now.

For Thine is the Kingdom the Power and the Glory, for ever and ever. Amen.

I got up.

The polisher turned and looked at me.

'Nice day,' she whispered.

'Yes.' I whispered back.

* * *

Snow is drifting down past the window, clinging to the creeper, muffling the intermittent sounds of passing cars. It taps from time to time like gentle fingers on the glass. I know the sound of each bell as it chimes each hour, St Bartholomew's, St Mary's, Anglesea Road, Haddington Road and, even if I am not too sunk in stupor, The Sacred Heart in Donnybrook.

* * *

He stopped typing. The silence was almost startling. The sound of the rhythmic tapping had merged with her thoughts, her breathing even, for the last couple of hours. She opened her eyes and looked up at the dazzling sky.

'I think, Irish woman . . .' She heard him push the chair back and the slapping noise made by his sandals on the tiled floor.

'. . . you should stay another week.'

She sat up and leaned her back against the iron railings and peered into the room. He was moving round the table putting his papers into neat piles, straightening the row of pencils and coloured pens that lay beside the typewriter.

'God, I'm hot,' she said. 'Roasted. I should have moved ages ago. I'm sure I've done myself a damage.'

'Perhaps even longer.'

'What?'

'You heard me.'

'Yes.'

'Then, what do you say?'

'Don't be silly.'

'What is silly about such a suggestion?'

'I have a job. I have to get back to my job.'

He walked over to the window and stood looking down at her.

'This job? What is this job?'

'You know quite well what it is, I've told you. I slog for an advertising agency. Big deal, big deal, big deal, but it pays the rent. We all have to be able to pay the rent.'

'Send them a telegram. Taken ill in Italy. Back three weeks. Keep seat warm. Amore.'

She laughed.

'Unfortunately they don't need me that much, amore or no amore. London is full of aspiring copy writers.'

'You should not be doing that. You should be doing better. Leave them.'

'Rent.'

'Pish to rent. You should try.'

'Try what?'

'Try harder, try more, Irish. You don't try. You are a very lazy person.'

'I'm a bit inadequate certainly, but . . .'

'Why you sat down when that man in blue say all that . . . rabbitch to you? Why you believed him?'

She didn't answer.

'Why you sat down?'

'If you can get through life sitting down, why bother standing up?'

'Foolishness. Joking. Flippant joking. You are always joking, Constance. I would like to see you cry.'

'Oh thanks.'

'I have concern for you.'

'Look here, Jacob, just because we're . . . we're here together like this doesn't give you any rights over me . . . doesn't mean . . . doesn't . . . Just mind your own bloody business. I live the way I want to live. I am the person I want to be.'

He smiled.

'That's true.' Her voice was sharp.

'Fanny hedgehog,' he said, still smiling. 'The first signs of trabble and you roll up into a ball and put your prickles out. No prickles, Irish. No quarrels. When it is so short a time we have together, there is no point to quarrel.'

He bent and kissed her cheek.

'Let us go and drink wine and eat calamares instead. No point to quarrel.'

*　　*　　*

I had always felt that after my mother's death I would find some kind of release, the awareness for the first time of an identity. It wasn't that we had been great friends or even communicated with each other in any important way. On the contrary I had always seemed to be a source of great irritation to her, a curious disappointment. The fact that I had been born the wrong sex had been the first major setback, from which our relationship never really recovered.

I felt angered as I walked among the cold tombstones, not only about the circumstances of her death but also that I still felt the same confusion inside myself that I always had. It was then in the flurry of windblown snow that the first thoughts came to me that I should have a child. I pushed the idea away. There in the landscape it seemed grotesque. I went home with Father and Bibi to hand round drinks and plates of savories to the family's mourning friends. That evening, slightly drunk and still wearing my black coat I boarded the B and I boat and went back to London.

*   *   *

Will this day ever become truly day? The heavy clouds squeeze the light away from between the sky and the earth. The flakes of snow twist monotonously through the air. The city smoke mingles with the clouds. In the day time you seldom hear the bells that chime so regularly through the night, chiming away your life.

'It's not a day for getting up at all.' Bridie pushed the door open with her knee and came in with a tray.

'All the world's lucky people are spending today in bed.'

She came over and put the tray beside me, edging it carefully through the books and papers, the boxes and bottles of pills, the empty glasses. A big blue satin bow tied her hair back from her face.

'Did you sleep well in your new room?'

'Like a log. Will I pour your tea?'

'No. I'll do it myself in a few minutes. I must go to the bathroom first. I hate cold tea.'

She helped me out of bed. I didn't like her touching me, hated the feeling that she might be contaminated by my decay.

When I came back from the bathroom she had made my bed and piled up a heap of pillows for me to lean into.

'It's a conspiracy,' I said.

'What's a conspiracy?'

'To keep me in bed all day. Who could resist a bed that looked as inviting as that?'

'I want to clean out the other room. Have it nice for Christmas.'

'How long till Christmas? What day is it today? I get so stupidly muddled.'

'Friday.'

I wondered if Jacob had received the letter. Perhaps it was following him round and round the world. London, Rome, Paris, New York. Maybe it would do that forever, always a step behind, Tel Aviv, Athens, anywhere except Berlin. On the other hand, maybe he had found it on his doormat yesterday or today and had read it and thrown it into the waste paper basket. He had every right to do that.

'Every right.'

'What's that?'

'I was just talking to myself. First sign of madness.'

If that were to be the case, the child would have every advantage. Every possible . . . A home, a family, a name, a certain sort of love, solid love. Yes. A God. Every advantage.

'Every advantage.'

'There's your tea now. Drink it up before it gets cold and stop muttering to yourself. Will you try a little piece of toast?'

She held out a plate to me that had four straight pieces of buttered toast on it.

I shook my head.

'I can't, Bridie, honestly. There's no point in my trying. I know what will happen. I'm sorry.'

'That's okay.'

'The tea is lovely. When did you say Christmas is?'

'Monday. Three more days.'

'Anyone at home?' shouted Bill's voice from the hall.

I laughed.

'That's the doctor. Such a silly question to ask. Tell him to come in. Maybe he'd like a cup of tea.'

'I'll get another cup.'

Bill came in, rather purple in the face.

'Good morning, patient.'

'Hello, Bill. This is Bridie, by the way. She's just going to get a cup for you. You look like a man in need of a cup of tea.'

'I sure am. Hello, Bridie. I'd really appreciate a cup of tea.'

She went out.

'It's a day would freeze the balls off you.'

He came over and stood looking down at me in his usual kindly and considering way.

'How's the patient?'

I laughed.

'I'm alive. I feel like Augustus who wouldn't eat his soup, though. Each time I look in the glass I see a little less substance, a little more shadow.'

He sat down beside me on the bed and took my wrist in his hand. I knew he was merely taking my pulse, but I felt a comfort just the same.

Bridie came in with a cup and saucer and put them down on the table.

Bill stared out of the window at the falling snow.

'Is there anything else you need?'

'No thanks, Bridie. I'll give a yell if there is.'

She went out, closing the door quietly behind her.

'She seems a nice girl.'

Gently, he let my hand fall on to the bedspread. He sighed and reached over to the teapot and poured himself a cup of tea.

'Will I last the day?'

'Fool. You really are a fool, Constance.'

'I have discovered that about myself. I am resigned in my declining moments to my own foolishness. Are you lonely?'

He looked a little startled, then fished a tealeaf out of his cup with the tip of his finger.

'I suppose so. Yes, indeed.' He laughed abruptly. 'Why do you always ask me things like that? Are you lonely?'

'I haven't time to be lonely. Here, have a piece of toast and make Bridie happy. There are a couple of things I'd like you to do for me. This seems a good time to mention them.' He took a piece of toast and nodded. 'One is the child ... don't look so alarmed. I'm not going to leave her to you in my will or anything like that. If ... or rather I should say when ... Jacob, her father comes. When he ... I want you to make sure that everything's all right. No nonsense from Bibi, that sort of thing.'

'Constance ...'

'No prevarication. I don't want things made difficult for him. Bibi needs an eye kept on her, you know that. He must be allowed to take the child away. She's his child after all. Bibi must have scruples ... purely kindness scruples ... but nonetheless. Just in case I'm not able ... I'm not around.'

Butter dribbled out of the corner of his mouth.

'You know what I mean?'

'Yes.'

'You'll see to it?'

'Yes.'

'Are you angry with me?'

'No.'

'I swear it's the right thing to do.'

'That's all right, Constance, I'll do whatever has to be done.'

'And the other thing ...'

'I love hot buttered toast. Why does nobody make hot buttered toast any more?'

'That must be cold buttered toast by now.'

'The other thing?'

He helped himself to another piece of toast.

'It may be a little more bother, but I would be very grateful. I've been writing this book . . . maybe it won't get completely finished . . . I can't cope with the typing any more, so it has disintegrated into long hand. Messy long hand. It may be dreadful. I don't know, because I'm too close to it. I'll never know. If you get it typed, tidy it up and send it to a publisher for me. A decent one . . . you know . . . Don't worry if they send it back with a little regretful note. You can forget it then. Jettison it. Would you mind? I'd like you to try. My posthumous glory.'

'Of course I don't mind. I'd be delighted to do that for you. What's it about?'

Everyone always asks that impossible question.

'A bear of very little brain.'

He grimaced, but made no comment.

'How long will it take you to finish it?'

His voice sounded faintly worried.

'Any time. Don't worry. A few days, a week. No need to worry. It's just something I promised myself I would try.'

He bent down and kissed my lank hair. If I didn't go soon, wherever I was going, I'd have no hair left. How humiliating that would be. Better dead than bald.

'Not too many aches and pains?' he asked in his professional voice.

'None that the whiskey won't cure.'

'I'd better be getting on with my calls. Would you like Angela to come and visit you?'

'No.'

He put his empty cup down on the tray and stood up.

'I don't mean to be rude. I just don't like to be interrupted.'

He picked up the pill bottle and looked at it, rolling it round in his fingers.

'Most of the chemists'll be shut over Christmas. I'll give the girl a prescription for some more of these. Just in case.'

'Thank you.'

'Goodbye, Constance. Don't worry about all those things. I'll see to them. I'll call back this evening. We'll have a drink together when my surgery is over.'

'I'd like that. I'll probably even get up. Dress up posh. Greet you in front of the Christmas tree, like a real person.'

'Goodbye.'

'Goodbye.'

*　*　*

'Did anything ever come of your writing?'

Her father always asked the same question at the same moment, just after they had ordered their meal and the menus had been removed by the waiter. A glass of pale sherry sat in front of each of them and candles flickered on the small table.

'Not really.'

She had never been able to bring herself to tell him about the interview with the man in the blue suit. She felt she didn't know him well enough to judge whether he would be amused, sympathetic or merely bored. He was mostly bored by their infrequent evenings together when he visited London. Perhaps bored was not quite the right word, uninterested might be more accurate.

'What a shame.' A smile moved his mouth.

I wonder if you love me, she thought as she looked carefully at his handsome, ageing face . . . love any of us . . . I don't just mean me . . . Would you have loved a son perhaps?

He raised the glass to his lips. Gold cufflinks, immaculate nails, the skin on the backs of his hands was beginning to wrinkle now, like well-worn gloves.

'Do you mind if I smoke?'

She shook her head. He took a gold case out of his pocket and opened it.

'I take it you haven't acquired the habit?'

'No.'

He took a cigarette from the case and laid it on the table beside the sherry glass and put the case away.

'I once thought seriously of becoming a writer myself.'

She looked at him with amazement as he lit his cigarette.

'Really, Father? When . . . ?'

'A long time ago. Yes. When I was at Cambridge I wrote a bit. Short stories.' He frowned, regretting, perhaps, his indiscretion. 'A play or two. That was my real interest, writing plays. Only for the university, you understand. I was very keen on theatre in those days.'

'Were they performed, your plays?'

'Oh yes.'

'I wish you'd told me before. Why didn't you?'

'It didn't seem very interesting. My personal failure . . . neither interesting nor inspiring in any way. Why did I tell you now, is really the question and I don't know the answer to that. It was a totally unpremeditated remark.'

'Why did you stop?'

He shrugged his shoulders slightly.

'I had to make decisions, my dear. The law seemed more secure. I have never been what you might call a daredevil.'

'And the stories . . . were they published?'

'Oh yes. Quite well received. The Strand . . . Blackwoods . . . you know . . . quite well . . .'

'Did Mother know?'

'I had made my decisions before I met your mother. I have never been quite sure whether or not I took the right decision. Over all, I think I did. Yes. I have had a few moments of regret, but only a few. I am not cut out for the artistic life.'

The waiter put two plates of smoked salmon down in front of them. Mr Keating pursed his lips in slight disapproval as he looked at the food.

'So,' he said as he picked up his knife and fork.

Constance watched him.

Carefully he dissected the salmon and put a piece in his mouth.

'I cannot imagine why a restaurant of this calibre gives its customers commercially smoked salmon. Taste it. Taste it.'

'It looks lovely,' said Constance.

'It's poor.' Peevishly he pushed his plate to one side.

'It's delicious, Father.'

'Poor. London has changed.'

'Well, I think it's delicious.'

'So . . .' He continued as if he had never interrupted himself in the first place '. . . it would have given me a certain satisfaction if you had become a writer. Had taken the idea seriously.'

'I did, do, take it seriously, Father. I just don't have the talent, or whatever you'd like to call it.'

'I would have got some pleasure from that all right. There's no denying that. I'm not, of course, suggesting that you and Barbara are not admirable. Admirable. Admirable.'

He obviously regretted his hasty treatment of the smoked salmon. He pulled the plate towards him and began to eat with speed.

'Talent, after all, has to be allied with so many other attributes; drive, persistence, egoism, commitment. I lacked the commitment. I was not prepared to fail. It seems that you, too, feel the same way.' He sprinkled a little red pepper on his salmon.

'A sad thing.'

He broke a piece of brown bread and popped it into his mouth.

'You look at your children as they grow, mature a bit, and will, yes, will, that somehow they will succeed in having some of the attributes that you yourself regret having lacked. At least . . .' he flushed away the painful taste of the smoked salmon with some sherry '. . . some development of the qualities that you find admirable in yourself. Is it a failure of some sort if you only see your own weaknesses in your children? I wonder.'

She felt the question was rhetorical and didn't say a word.

'Your mother would have preferred that I became a judge, but I had no interest, I turned it down. I preferred the bar to the bench. Yes indeed. You and Barbara . . .'

'Bibi and I are all right, Father.'

'You are all right.'

There was a certain contempt in his voice.

'We are the way we want to be. Isn't that all right? As you are. We chose.'

He shook his head.

The waiters surrounded the table. Plates, glasses, knives danced across the white cloth.

'Can I ask you one thing?'

He bent his head slightly, saying neither yes, nor no.

'I've always wondered why, when it wasn't really necessary, you went to the war. It might have ruined your career . . . Mother said . . . some people might have taken it amiss. Mother . . .'

'Your mother always believed in people keeping their feet on the ground.'

'It's just something I have always wondered about.'

She paused and looked at his face. He was escaping from her. She put out a hand as if she might be able to catch some part of him, but laid it down again on the cloth among the glasses and the silver.

'After all, you said yourself, only a moment ago, that you weren't a daredevil.'

His voice was matter-of-fact once more.

'It wasn't that I objected to De Valera's neutrality in any way. On the contrary. It would have been insanity to hurl such a new-born state, and one born out of such pain, into a major war. Insanity. I did, however, feel that I had a duty to perform . . . don't get me wrong, I had no political feelings of being West British or anything like that, no Crown fever . . . I suppose it was a feeling of duty that I had learnt at school. At Cambridge.'

He sighed.

The waiter poured a few drops of wine into his glass and waited, bottle poised, beside him. He took up the glass and looked at the wine for a moment before touching it briefly with his lips. He nodded to the waiter.

'It was a very personal decision . . . to defend, in my own small way, democracy. I know it has its faults. There are many who would totally condemn it, but it was the one thing that gave us, you understand, the freedom to remain neutral, gave me the freedom to choose. So I chose to go. I think it was the right choice. There was a time when we all felt very depressed. You wouldn't remember. You were too young. But there was a time when it seemed possible that Hitler might win. So.'

He picked up his glass and had a drink.

'I wasn't a hero in any way. I can assure you of that. Now that claret is truly excellent.'

He had said too much and the rest of the meal was eaten mostly in silence.

* * *

The telephone bell was ringing. I listened for a moment and then began to struggle out of bed. The bell stopped and I heard Bridie's voice talking in the other room. I had forgotten about her. I lay back into the pillows. After a little while she came into the room.

'It was Mrs Barry on the phone. She gave me a list for shopping.'

'She would.'

'And the doctor told me to get pills. I could go and do that now if it suits you.'

'I'll be fine. Look . . . would you go into town for me and get me a present for the baby? I'd better get something for her . . . after all . . .'

'Of course I'll do that.'

'I've no ideas. What on earth do you give a baby? Get something nice. Something you think a baby would like.'

She smiled.

'Take some money from the drawer. Take fifty pounds.'

She went across the room and opened the drawer.

'Will you be all right if I am away a couple of hours?'

'Of course I'll be all right. Pour me out a large glass of whiskey before you go and shove me over those notebooks and pens. Lady Muck I am, every comfort. Thank you.'

'Mrs Barry says she mightn't get round today. She'll do her best, but you'll understand if she doesn't. The children all send their love and they hope to see you tomorrow.'

'Yes. Don't rush back from town, Bridie. I want you to tell me what Grafton Street looks like and what carols they're singing and I'd like you to get a present for yourself.'

'I . . .'

'Something you'd really like. I'm sorry to ask you to do it, but there doesn't seem to be any alternative. If I asked Bibi to do it, she'd be bound to get you something sensible. I'd like you to get something that you can look at in twenty years and remember your first Christmas in freedom.'

She nodded.

'Perhaps you should take some more money.'

'I'll do no such thing.' Her voice sounded shocked.

'And don't go feeling you should get something for me. That would be truly silly.'

'A book . . .'

'I have no time to read books any more.'

'A bottle of whiskey?'

I laughed.

'Away. Away, cheeky child. I've enough whiskey here to drown in, if I feel that way inclined.'

* * *

'It's a lovely little baby girl.'

Constance opened her eyes with caution. Someone was speaking to her.

'A lovely little baby girl. All in good working order. Do look, Mummy, do look.'

A nurse dangled something in front of Constance's face.

Constance turned her head away and shut her eyes again.

'Not now,' she said. 'Just take it away. For a while, half an hour or so.'

The lovely little baby girl squalled at the words, but the nurse's footsteps and the squalling moved away. Constance tried to bury herself in sleep. Sleep was evasive. Poor father. Well, why after all do you say poor father? Feet hurried in the corridor. To die at the age of sixty-eight, still in your prime, hale if not hearty. Just to be dead one morning in your bed, the sheets unruffled by spasms of pain or anxiety. A door opened and quietly closed. Daffodils, she had said to Bibi on the dreadful telephone. Lots and lots of daffodils.

'But why can't you come over, Constance? Why?'

So there he was, lying forever beside the woman he didn't love. So many people must suffer the same fate . . . little pains still grasped at her guts. She turned restlessly. Elusive sleep. Strange lonely Father, whom would you have preferred to have beside you for eternity? Neither Bibi nor I, that's for sure. In some distant place, a baby cried. Some companion from your war years perhaps? Or Cambridge, when you made your decision . . . right or wrong?

'You never come over when you are needed. But, honestly . . . now, of all times . . . now . . . Constance . . . What will I say to people?'

Remote shadow man, for whom I felt no recognisable love, no hate and now can feel no regret. In other circumstances, I would have stood beside your grave and sung those hymns in the echoing church; walked once more along the ghost-lined path. You would smile and understand and go away.

'You might at least think of me, the support I need, even if you have no feelings for poor Father.'

He would have been a beautiful corpse; his body barely thickened by age, the angularity of his face softened slightly. I wonder if they buried him in his morning clothes. He always looked his best in them.

'You're going to what? A what? You're joking, Constance. I really don't believe you. This is the last blooming straw.'

She opened her eyes, exasperated by her recollections and looked up at the ceiling. It wasn't much to look at.

'Would you like to see the baby now?' asked a voice from the other side of the room.

'Am I awake?'

'Yes. At last. You've been asleep for ages.'

'I was having a dream . . . a nightmare . . . horrible confusion. I'm glad I'm awake now.'

'It's the anaesthetic. It does that to a lot of people. It makes some people sick. Do you want to hold her?'

'Oh . . . yes. I suppose I should.'

The nurse came over and settled the pillows behind her.

'I feel very stiff.'

'You'll be as right as rain in a day or two.'

She bent down and picked up a white wrapped object from a cradle at the end of the bed.

'I brought her back from the nursery. I thought you'd wake soon and want to see her.'

She put the package into Constance's arms. Constance looked with apprehension at the red wrinkled face, at one tiny clenched fist. A fuzz of black hair stood up around the worried forehead.

'Is she all right? I mean . . . ?'

'All in good working order. No problems. A lovely little girl.'

'She doesn't look a bit lovely to me. She looks . . .'

'She's beautiful. You should see some of them. Give her a day or two and you'll see how beautiful she is.'

'She looks . . .'

She looked, not very surprisingly, the image of Jacob Weinberg. Jacob taken and boiled in a huge pot until shrunken and reddened by cooking and then taken out and wrapped in a white cloth.

Constance began to laugh.

She handed the baby back to the nurse.

'Thank God,' she said. 'She doesn't look like my father.'

'Her father,' corrected the nurse.

'No. No. My father. She doesn't look a bit like my father. I was afraid I might have given birth to a ghost.'

'She's a little pet. Mummy's little pet.'

'That remains to be seen. I think I'll sleep again for a while, before she and I really come to grips with each other.'

*   *   *

'You are so lucky, Irish.'

'What's so lucky about me?'

The whole world was below them. A beautiful, blue plate, deepening to a dark, almost indigo rim around the edge, glazed by the sun. In the centre, down the hill from where they were sitting, the houses were like tiny white boxes, piled along the edge of the sea. The smell of the dry grass and the flowers was warm and very sweet.

'You carry nothing. You are one of the few people that I have ever met who carries nothing. I feel I have two thousand years of history tied to my back. A heavy load. I have tried so hard to throw it off . . . when first I came to England. After that, as I grew, became a man . . . I tried so hard to become a new, fresh, person . . . someone untouched by history, but it couldn't happen, no matter how hard I tried, it couldn't happen. Now, each day I feel so heavy with the burden. I hear all the time so many voices in my head. We have so little time and I must creep through it. A snail. You carry nothing.'

Cicadas ticked in the silence, like a million busy clocks. Lizards basked on the rocks, darting tongues flicked as they moved over the scrub.

She smiled a nervous, darting smile.

'I never wanted burdens. No pain. They could have bruised my shoulders. You just have to look around and you see so much pain. I've never wanted any part of that. You can get through life without it, if you hold yourself together. That's why I must go back to my job. My groove . . . self-made. God knows what would happen to me if I stepped out of my groove.'

'Try.'

'Don't be daft. Throw away all those years of digging my groove? You'd really like to see me out there in the cold?'

'Yes.'

'There's friendship for you.'

'Yes.'

Far away a vapour trail stained the perfection of the sky.

'I hate all this blue. After a while I long for a cloud or two. Don't you? One little black cloud would be nice.'

'Just one little black cloud here means thunder, lightning, storms, earth tremors and volcanic eruptions. Would you wish all that on these happy people?'

She laughed.

'Almost. To break the tedium, damage all this boring blue.'

'What colour are the skies in your groove?'

'Grey. A nice, dim and peaceful grey.'

* * *

I remember only two white Christmases in all the forty-five through which I have lived. In spite of those Christmas cards we inflict on each other, all snow and stars and trees weighted with diamond icicles. Only two. One of them was in London, not so many years ago when the snow turned after twenty-four hours to brown mud, which was swept into the gutters and froze, making high impassable mounds between the pavement and the road. The giant red buses really came into their own, I remember, moving masses of colour, the only colour in the permanent twilight of those few weeks. The weight of snow, lying for a couple of weeks on the roof of my bathroom, cracked three panes of glass and several buckets and a plastic bowl had to be deployed to catch the torrents when the thaw began.

The other white Christmas was so far back in my life that I only have most unsatisfactory memories of my joy at finding the garden smooth and sparkling; no flower beds, no tennis court, no paths, no neatly dug and waiting vegetable garden, just this, vast, it seemed, expanse of untouched white, not quite untouched, but gently patterned by the tiny criss-cross marks of birds' feet. The high escallonia hedges, protecting us from our neighbours, had become white walls overnight, and sighed uneasily from time to time under their burden of snow. It must have been during the war, and my father home on leave, because we walked to church, all four of us, and our feet crunched through the snow and left beautiful, clean, deep footmarks. My mother wore a fur hat that made her look like a princess in a Russian fairy story. She complained because the snow seeped its way through the soles of her shoes, and she had to sit in church with cold damp feet. Father told her she should have worn her boots. The bells sounded so clearly that day, it was as if I had never heard them before. Everyone seemed happy, but I don't suppose they were.

Even the pen feels so heavy now, it tires my fingers to push it across the page. Mother sits by my bed from time to time dressed as if she were about to go out to play bridge, her suede-gloved hands clasped on her knee, her bag beside her, waiting for some bell to ring, some knock to come on the door. I hope she isn't waiting for me. I would hate to start whatever existence there may be in front of me at one of Mother's bridge parties.

Bridie must have come in without my hearing her. Maybe I had slept for a little while without noticing. I can hear water running in the kitchen and the squeak of the refrigerator door being opened and closed.

I have a black silk dress with buttons down the front. I think that with a secret use of pins and its wide silk sash, I might be able to wear it and not look too painful. As if it mattered. Such foolishness we all indulge in at curious moments.

'What do you be writing all the time?'

'Oh, Bridie, hello. Where has the time gone to. It seems to me only about fifteen minutes since you went out.'

'I've brought you a cup of tea. Would you like anything to eat? I've made scrambled egg for myself and there's fruit and cheese.'

'Perhaps I'll try an apple. Bring yours in and eat it here and tell me what you've been doing.'

When she left the room to collect the food I poured a large measure of whiskey into the tea. That way it didn't have to make her feel uneasy. She handed me an apple on a plate and a knife and then sat down by the bed with the tray on her knee.

'If you don't mind me asking . . . what is it you do be writing at . . . so much of the time?'

'Nothing really very interesting. I always wanted to write a book and didn't seem to get down to it properly. Better late than never. There is one important thing though . . . I want you to gather it all up, all the notebooks and the bits of paper . . . everything and give them to Bill . . . the doctor. What is important is that you don't let Bibi get her hands on it. Bill knows about it. He'll look after it. She might just throw it all away, something like that. You'll rescue it for me . . . won't you, the moment you think it's necessary?'

She nodded.

'A book. A story. Is it a good story?'

'It's not much of a story. No plot, no adventures, no love. Not much to recommend it, I'm afraid. Bibi might be right to throw it away.'

'Or she might be wrong.'

I laughed.

'That's something I'll never know.'

'Eat your apple.'

'Right, nurse.'

'If you don't eat anything at all you won't live to finish it . . . the book.'

I cut a small piece of apple and put it into my mouth. My jaws ached as I tried to chew. I doubted if I would get through very much of it.

'Tell me about town . . .'

'Gorgeous. Terribly cold, but there I was like a rich lady with all that money in my pocket and I hardly felt the cold at all. I gave fifty pence to some carol singers. I hope you don't mind?'

'Not a bit.'

'I hope these are all right.'

She handed me a paper bag with two small boxes inside. I pulled one out and opened it. Two hands held a crowned heart up for me to see. I took the ring out of the box and looked at it in the palm of my hand.

'It's lovely. A lovely present.'

'They're both the same. One of the teachers had one and I always used to think that I'd like one for myself. I hope that's all right. I thought the baby might like to have one too, when she's older that is, of course. It's an Irish ring, you know? That's what my teacher told me anyway. You'd better not give it to the baby too soon, she might swallow it.'

'Here.' I held the ring out to her. 'Put it on. Have it now. There's no point in being silly about this. Wear it now. Happy Christmas, Bridie.'

She took it from me and put it on her right hand. She sat looking at it for a long time.

'I'd like to be happy,' she said eventually. 'I'd really like to be happy.' I touched her hand.

'You must always believe in the possibility. If you do that . . . you never know . . . you never know. It looks nice on you. You've got long fingers. Some people can't wear big rings like that.'

'It didn't look nice on Miss O'Toole. But the other . . . I hope that pleases you. I can bring it back. The man in the shop said I could bring it back.'

'No, I'm delighted. She'll be delighted too . . . if she doesn't swallow it.'

Bridie laughed.

'I don't know why I said such a silly thing. Sometimes words pop out of my mouth without me having thought of them at all. Sister always used to tell me to think before I spoke. I do try, but it doesn't always work.'

I cut another piece of apple and put it in my mouth. Needle-like pains shot up through my gums when I tried to chew. I spat the apple out on to the plate.

'I can't.'

'Some toast? There's some chicken out there. A nice little bit of chicken?'

'No. I'm sorry, Bridie. You're not to worry. I can't have you around if you're going to worry. I just can't eat. That's all. There's no point in trying.'

'Couldn't they feed you in some way.'

'They could. They could stick tubes up my nose and needles into my arm. They could open me up and take bits out of me. They could strap me to a bed and keep me alive for six months, or even perhaps a year, but . . . I'd rather go in my own time, not theirs. Don't you bloody worry, or you'll have to find yourself another job.'

She nodded.

'Sorry,' I said.

She nodded again.

'I'll make a little Christmas parcel out of this. There should be lots of wrapping paper somewhere. Mother always used to keep it in a drawer. Then we'll hang it on the tree. You'll make sure she gets it, won't you?'

'Yes.'

'I think I'll get up when I've finished my tea. Would you be very kind and turn on the bath for me?'

She got up and moved towards the door.

'Oh . . . and Bridie . . .'

'Yes?'

'If you go through the door beyond the kitchen and down the stairs you'll find what remains of my father's wine cellar. If you could manage to find a couple of bottles of champagne, you might bring them up. I think we'll have a celebration this evening. You and I and the doctor. Might as well go out with a bang as a whimper. I don't see why I should leave Father's champagne for Bibi.'

'Champagne.'

'The Christmas drink.'

'Champagne.'

'And we'll celebrate the end of your first twenty-four hours of freedom.'

'They'd summon me back if they only knew.'

*   *   *

Constance dropped the letter from Bibi unopened in the waste paper basket on her way to collect the baby's bottle from the fridge. She lit the gas and stood the bottle in a saucepan of water. It was odd how the flat no longer felt the same now that there was another inmate. The sounds and smells were different. The furniture had been rearranged; there was different food in the refrigerator. It was no longer her private shell. While she waited for the bottle to heat she walked across the room and took the letter out of the basket again. She opened the envelope and pulled out three closely written pages. Bibi's writing was like her face, neat, precise, symmetric, no blemishes. She didn't mince her words. She was relieved that neither of their parents were alive to be troubled and grieved by the irresponsible behaviour of their daughter. It was typical of you never to think of the feelings of others. You are like a child, some Peter Pan character, who had never bothered to grow up. Selfish, selfish, selfish and, of course, deeply irresponsible. Yes, she was repeating that word, stressing it. Irresponsible. Had it never occurred to you what sort of a life a child born in such circumstances would be likely to have. Liberation, freedom, big words, but words used too much and too frequently as excuses for self-indulgence. And what about the father? Who was he? Was he intending to support his child? Presumably the thought of marriage is out of the question . . . too easy a solution . . . and so on and so on.

Constance opened the cupboard beneath the sink and dropped the letter into the bin among the orange peels and the yogurt cartons. She picked the bottle out of the saucepan and shook it. She felt so tired. A slight pain nagged at the base of her spine. Dear Bibi, she wrote in her mind, shaking a drop of milk on to the back of her hand, I'm sorry I took your letter out of the waste paper basket, sorry I opened it, sorry I read it. She stood the bottle back in the hot water again. If it was too cold they got colic and screamed for hours. If it was too hot they wouldn't drink the damn stuff. I'm sorry I had to shock your system so drastically. I'm sorry our father died peacefully in his sleep two weeks ago, I'm sorry I wasn't able to get to the funeral, I'm sorry my existence causes you such pain and anguish. Sorry, sorry, sorry. That should be all right now, blood heat. The same heat night or day, winter or summer, like mother's milk pumping out of the breast, guaranteed pure, free from additives. Now with both our parents gone, dear sister, we have no one to protect us from death, so we should be kind to each other. Yours ever, Constance. P.S. Care a little, that's all. Just care a little.

*　*　*

The bus joggled away from them in a cloud of pale dust, down a twisting hill towards a distant cluster of houses on the edge of the sea. They stood for a moment and watched the dust settle on the vines and on the fig trees that bordered the road.

'Well,' she said. She already felt crushed by the heat.

'It's a sort of mad dogs and Englishmen situation, isn't it?'

'We walk, Irish.'

'Or we sit under that tree and wait for the bus to come back.'

'We walk. We eat too much. We drink too much. We lie in the sun and snore too much. Now we must walk.'

'It's going to be very hot.'

'It's going to be very good for us.'

'You have the wrong attitude to holidays. You're supposed to return to work exhausted with pleasure. Physically tanned and mentally stupefied.'

'Not for me. I do not know holidays. Sometimes I work in the grey melancholy of London, then one day I buy a ticket and move somewhere else to work. Italy maybe, France, New York. Like a migrating bird. I need it to be like that. Come, we walk. There is no point to wait for the bus. We walk, we sweat out of us all that food and drink, so with a clear conscience we can start again.'

'I have to go so soon. I have no time to start again.'

'That is your choice. You have your rules of living, I have mine . . . Walk, Irish woman. We will then have circumnavigated the island. You must always do that with an island.'

He took her arm and they began to walk along the road, the way the bus, which didn't feel the need to circumnavigate the island, would not be going.

'It's amazing,' she said after a while. 'How olive trees always look a million years old.'

'They are a million years old.'

'But they can't all be. Someone must surely be planting new ones, like the year before last, or even the century before last. Think of all the children even, on this island alone, who must be popping olive stones into the ground daily.'

'Mediterranean children are not so foolish as Irish children, or even English children.'

'But what will happen when one day in another million years or so all the olive trees in the world die of extreme old age? That has to happen sometime. Just in the natural course of things.'

'No more olive trees. Olives finish.'

He made a dramatic gesture with his hands. All the olives vanished from the earth. No more stuffed olives in jars on the shelves of supermarkets, no more olives in American dry martinis, no more olive oil.

'I don't suppose civilisation will end with the olive.'

'It could though, Irish, end before the olive.'

She laughed.

They walked.

'Will you ever go back to Poland?'

There were low stone walls on either side of them. Below them, a pattern of walls and vine-filled fields fell away towards the distant sea.

'No,' he said after a long silence. 'There are many ifs. If I were young I might go. If I didn't remember so much, so many dead people. If I had in front of me more future than past. I have spent so long, all these years, trying to pretend that I could become something other than what I am.'

'British . . . like you said to me when we met . . . remember . . . last week or whenever it was?'

'That is my choke.'

'It's not a very good joke.'

'It is a more respectable label than . . .'

'Than what?'

'A wandering Chew.'

'What about Israel? You could go and live there.'

He laughed.

'Ah no, Irish. I have none of that dedication. I have no love for politics of that kind. Beside, I am a north European, like you I find the sun dismal after a while. Too, I find that militant idealism very dismal . . . more than dismal. It appalls me. No matter what different names it gives itself, flags it waves, it is the same. The honourable justification of violence will always be to me the greatest evil, because it makes men blind.'

A small grey van hurtled past them, drowning them in dust.

'I haven't got the courage to look at my own ghosts. If I had children . . . then it would be different. I would take them back to smell the earth and the stones and the rivers . . . walk in the forests. I would have to talk to my ghosts again, but for me . . . for me alone it is not worth the pain.'

They walked in silence for a while, kicking the dust up in little spurts as they moved their feet.

'If you have never known anguish you can never understand it, understand . . . how people can be scarred by it. Perhaps we should all have died and then in time the world could have forgotten. Honourably forgotten. Those of us who remain prick constantly at the conscience of the world . . . We embarrass everyone by our survival.'

'Oh come on . . .'

'It's true. No point to argue.'

'I won't argue. It's too hot to argue. If we were doing this walk at home, there would be a pub at every bend in the road.'

'The Irish drink too much. It is a well-known fact.'

'A well-known myth. We also keep pigs in the kitchen and have leprechauns at the bottom of the garden.'

'What is a . . . leprechaun? That is something of which I have never heard.'

'A fairy shoemaker. A doer of mischief . . . and closely connected with equally mythical pots of gold. A sort of hobgoblin. I think that would be the English equivalent.'

'A hopgoplin.'

Constance laughed.

'Why are you laughing?'

'You have some lovely words.'

In spite of the heat and dust she did a little dance.

'I am deeda a hopgoplin, dancing to the tunes of Scott Joplin deeda I wear a coat of green poplin and I'm going to cast a spell upon you ooo. Oh Lord I am hot. Why are we doing this?'

'I have told you. So that we may sweat and be healthy. My father always taught us it was our duty to be healthy. He really believed in the *mens sana in corpore sano* idea. He used to take us for long walks through the gardens and by the lakes of Wilanow. Each morning that would be, very very early, before we would go to school. Then he would go home to practise his piano. Every day he would play four hours . . . sometimes more. Sometimes of course he would be away giving recitals, concerts, here, there and . . . then the flat was silent and I have to say we didn't take our early morning walks. My mother did not have the same force of character. Promise me, she would say when she came to say goodnight, promise me you'll take your walk tomorrow morning, and we would say yes, Mamma, we promise.'

He pushed his hands deep down into his trouser pockets and walked in silence.

'Well?' she asked after a while. 'Did you?'

He shook his head.

'So now you're taking it out on me.'

'In the summer the windows of his studio were wide, wide open and the people who lived around would come and sit in their gardens and listen to him play. Chopin, the great Beethoven piano sonatas, Brahms, Liszt. We used to get so tired of his music and say, Father, play us something good. Something we can enjoy. Something that is fun. It was your Scott Joplin that reminded me. If we had been good, learnt our lessons, not been too annoying to our mother, he would sit down and shake his wrists and play for us. He always shook his wrists before he played. It was as if he were shaking all the other things of the world off his hands, leaving only the music.'

In the distance a dog barked. A flurry of irrelevant sound.

'They killed him first.'

'I . . .'

'I have only heard from others who were there, other Chews who were servants in the camp. There were some who did that, you understand, in the hope for survival.'

She nodded.

'The commandant was a great lover of music. A man, so they said, of discernment and sensitivity.'

He smiled faintly as he said the words.

'He was to give this party in his home. They came to my father and said he was to play the piano. I remember. He looked at his hands and said how could he play after so long without practice. They brought him to a room every day for three weeks where there was a piano, a beautiful Steinway concert grand. And they gave him food so that he would regain some strength, and for those three weeks he practised. Beethoven, they told him, was what the Commandant wanted him to play, and some Schumann. They gave him what music he wanted. For those three weeks he lived in a world of joy. His face became alive again. He didn't seem to see or understand what was going on around him at all. The only reality was the room with the Steinway.'

A mangy looking dog lying in the shade of an olive tree lifted its head and looked at us as we went past. He was too hot to do more than give a warning growl in our direction. Below in a field his master was trimming his vines.

'The evening came for the concert and after that we never saw him again.'

'What happened?'

'Well, they say, and it may be myth, like your hopgoplins, that he went into the big room to play. There were officers and their wives. A few local big-wigs, collaborators, whatever you like to call them. My father was dressed somehow into evening clothes. He walked straight to the piano and sat down. I can see him sitting there shaking his wrists. They said he played a couple of chords and then softly music came from his finger, they never told me what it was, and he spoke. He spoke in German so that they could understand. By the rivers of Babylon, there we sat down, yea and we wept, when we remembered Zion. We hanged our harps upon the willows in the midst thereof. For there they that carried us away captive required of us a song; and they that wasted us required of us mirth, saying sing us one of the songs of Zion. How shall we sing the Lord's song in a strange land? If I forget thee, O Jerusalem let my right hand forget her cunning. If I do not remember thee let my tongue cleave to the roof of my mouth; if I prefer not Jerusalem above my greatest joy. O daughter of Babylon who art to be destroyed; happy shall he be that rewardeth thee as thou hast served us. Happy shall he be that taketh and dasheth thy little children against the stones.'

Damn, she thought, oh damn, oh damn.

'I don't suppose they let him finish it.'

He gave an odd little bow towards her as if to thank her for her patience.

'First I believe they shut his hands under the lid of the piano and broke them into bits. I don't know any more. Even that story may not be true. We never saw him again. Not long after they took my mother and my two sisters. Some people say he was a fool. Yes. A fool.'

Damn, damn.

'Psalm, a hundred and twenty-seven,' she heard her voice say.

He smiled at her and took her hand for a moment in his.

'No one has to say anything. There is nothing to be said. They are my ghosts. I must live with them.'

'I really wish you hadn't told me that.'

'That, Irish, is what they all say.'

* * *

If I could choose I would die in the bath. Just drift, lapped by warm sweet water, into nothing. Dark. It seems to us it must be dark. Peace anyway. A most agreeable thought. I don't wash much any more, just lie there and let my pain seep into the water and then gurgle away down the plug hole. A temporary remission.

* * *

'I'm afraid Mrs . . . ah . . .'

'Miss,' she reminded him.

'Miss Keating. The news . . . I have to tell you . . . I'm afraid, it's not too good.'

'Oh.'

Constance was mildly startled.

This time there were no pigeons on his window sill, only grey wet London roofs under the grey wet London sky outside the window. He shifted the papers on his desk. Why, she wondered, am I constantly having confrontations with men behind desks?

'It's not the child, I hope? There's nothing wrong with her, is there?'

'No. No. No.' His voice was reassuring. 'She's a fine healthy baby. No cause for alarm in that direction at all. But that last blood test of yours . . .' He paused and looked at her, wondering to himself what sort of person she was. A person for lies, or the truth.

'Well?'

Hell, she thought, anaemia, iron injections, pills, liver twice a week for life. I hate liver.

'It's nothing serious, I hope? I'm expected back at work next week.'

'I'm afraid it is.'

She looked at him with surprise.

He took the bull by the horns.

'Leukemia actually.' He looked down at his papers again.

She burst out laughing for a moment, and then stopped. He wasn't a joking sort of a man.

'There must be some mistake.'

He shook his head.

'I'm afraid . . .'

'But I don't feel ill. I feel great. I mean, shouldn't I feel something . . . have symptoms?'

'You have.'

He smoothed the evidence with his fingers.

'I see.'

There was a very long silence. As she stared out at the wet roofs, her heart began to hammer at her ribs with a ferocity she had never known before. She put out a hand to touch the desk in front of her, to feel its solidity. She waited with her fingers on the cool wood for the hammering to subside.

'You're an obstetrician,' she said finally.

He smiled.

'That's true. But if it hadn't been for your post-natal check up this mightn't have been discovered until . . .'

'Isn't it always too late with leukemia?'

'We can prolong life expectancy.'

She nodded.

'As you so rightly say, this is not my field, but I have arranged for you to see a specialist. He will advise you as to what is best to do. You had better make arrangements for the child. I would imagine you will be admitted into hospital straight away. Mr Leeson is a very good man, will see you tomorrow morning at eleven. There's no point in delaying.'

'All the little white cells are eating all the little red ones?'

'Something along those lines.'

'How long have they been at it? Isn't it odd that I never even suspected that this sort of ... well, genocide was going on inside me? I have been very tired, yes. But I put that down to the baby. How long ... ?'

'I don't know. You must ask Mr Leeson all these questions. There was no sign of anything untoward when we originally took a blood test.'

'No. No. I don't mean that. I mean, how long?' She lifted her hand from the desk and pointed towards the future.

He shrugged.

'Mr Leeson. There are all sorts of new drugs, new forms of therapy. Who can tell? And there are remissions, times when the activity is slowed down.'

'I don't want to know about all those speculative experiments. How long, at worst? That's what I want to know.'

'Mr Leeson.'

He was beginning to look anxious.

'Just forget Mr Leeson for the moment and tell me straight. There are all sorts of decisions I have to make.'

'I suppose ... you should wait till ...'

'Let's leave Mr Leeson out of it. You have just told me that I'm going to die. I only want you . . . you to tell me when.'

'I can't possibly tell you that. I don't know. Nobody knows these things. It could just happen any time. You could . . . em . . . last up to a year.'

'Out and about?'

'I don't know. It's not for me to say. Weeks, months. It's . . .' his voice tailed away, '. . . in the lap of the gods.'

'It's crazy, quite . . . crazy. I had made plans for the next twenty-five years.'

'I'm . . .'

'I suppose it's tempting fate to regard the future as a right.'

'. . . sorry.'

'No. You shouldn't have to say that. I'm sorry you had to tell me such lugubrious news.'

She stood up and held her hand out towards him across the desk.

'I'll say goodbye . . . and of course thank you. I don't suppose we'll be seeing each other again. You'll send me your account, won't you? Promptly.'

She smiled at him as she said the word.

He stood up and came round the desk. He took her hand. His hand was cold and very smooth and clean. Pumice and a nail brush several times a day, soft handtowels and expensive soap. Perhaps a touch of disinfectant now and then, but not so that it was noticeable.

'Mr Leeson will report to me on your progress, Mrs . . .'

'Miss.'

'I'm sorry.'

'I think perhaps it would be best if you were to cancel the appointment you so kindly made for me.'

'I hardly . . .'

'You see, I think I'll go home. To Dublin. I think that would be the best thing to do. My father's house . . . well, I think . . . it's empty. He . . . ah . . . It's been empty a little while now. We were going to sell it, my sister and I, but now . . . now I think we might put it off for a little while. I think . . .'

She turned abruptly and walked towards the door. 'Thank you for all you've done for me . . . and of course the child. I don't mean to be rude. I just think it's better to go home. I'd hate to be buried in a London cemetery surrounded by all those people I've never heard of.'

'Miss Keating.'

He came towards her with an envelope in his hand.

'You'll be needing these. My report, the X rays, all that sort of thing. You should show them to your doctor. As soon as possible. I would advise expedition.'

He looked at her curiously for a moment.

'You're not expecting a miracle of some sort to happen, are you?'

'Yes, I think I am.'

'I . . .'

'Not the miracle you mean. Don't worry. A private and personal internal miracle. Nothing to do with living to a ripe old age, confounding medical opinion. Nothing like that at all.'

She gave an odd little bow in his direction.

'Goodbye.'

'Goodbye, Miss Keating. Mmmm . . . and good luck.'

* * *

The lights on the tree looked gay and elegant. Bridie had bought some gold chrysanthemums and put them in a bowl on the table. It looked like a party. Even the black dress didn't look too bad. I had trouble with my shoes though. For some reason my feet won't hold together in high-heeled shoes, so I was obliged to wear my slippers. I told Bridie where to find the champagne glasses and she was getting them when Bill walked into the room. He looked tired. He smiled as he looked around the room and came over and kissed my hand.

'How splendid everything is looking . . . and you, Constance.'

'Scarecrow.'

'You're not scaring this crow.'

'That's just because I'm an inefficient scarecrow.'

'How are you feeling?'

'Bloody. But we're going to have champagne and then I'll feel great.'

Bridie came in with the glasses and put them on the table.

'Good evening, Doctor.'

'Good evening, Bridie. You've done wonders around here.'

'I like a place to look nice.'

'Quite right. Quite right.'

'Will I get the champagne from the fridge?'

'A bottle. Yes, please. I hope you've brought a glass for yourself. You must have some with us.'

She left the room.

'Has Barbara been today?'

'No. She has a lot to do. Now that Bridie's here, she knows that I'm all right.'

He nodded.

'She rang me again. She still thinks that you should go into hospital.'

'What did you say?'

'I said you might as well stay here now. There seemed very little point in upsetting you.'

'Thanks, pal. What did she say to that?'

'There wasn't much she could say. I am, after all, your doctor. She, also . . .'

'There,' said Bridie arriving in with the bottle in her hand. She put it down by the glasses and admired it for a moment. 'Doesn't it look great?'

Bill picked it up and took the gold foil off the cork.

'Let's see if it tastes good. God, I need a drink. Terrible need.'

'Would you rather have whiskey. I don't want to rail-road . . .'

He shook his head. His thumbs worked hard. He gritted his teeth. Bridie watched as the cork began to move.

Pop.

'A glass, quick.'

'Oh. Oh. Oh.'

'You shall have the honour of the first sip.'

He handed her the frothing glass. Apprehensively she sipped and then sneezed.

'Oh.'

Bill laughed. I laughed. She sneezed and laughed too.

For a moment we were held together in a bubble of curious happiness. It hadn't existed a minute before and would undoubtedly evaporate before long, leaving us without any comprehension as to why it had happened, what chemistry had occurred.

'It's all those blue lights on the tree,' said Bill, rather obscurely answering a question that no one had asked. He sat down abruptly and stared at me.

'You do look nice,' he said at last.

I smiled at him.

'I think I'll run up to Donnybrook Church, if it's all right with you. I might get confession.'

'You run along, Bridie. That's fine with me.'

'I won't be long.'

'Don't worry, Bridie,' said Bill. 'I'll look after her. Away you go and confess your terrible sins. Champagne and all.'

She sneezed again.

'I'll leave the rest till I get back. I might be falling all over the place.'

'Wrap up well or you might freeze to death. Say a prayer for us.'

'I will. Oh I will.'

She went out, closing the door quietly behind her.

'A nice girl,' said Bill.

'I hope I don't expect too much of her. Exploit her in any way. I can feel myself relying on her more and more.'

'She's young and good-hearted and it . . .'

'Won't be for too long.'

He nodded abruptly and took a mouthful of champagne.

'Sorry,' he said. 'I shouldn't . . .'

'It's all right. It doesn't worry me. What's the use of worrying dee da deea dee da, so . . . What else was Bibi on about?'

'The child.'

'Of course. I should have known. I do hope she's not going to be difficult.'

'You do keep throwing terrible problems at people, Constance, and then ducking out yourself, saying things like, I do hope she's not going to be difficult . . . leaving other people to make very hard decisions.'

'That's not true. I'm making decisions all the time. It's just that nobody else likes my decisions. I'm here. That's my decision, not where you all wanted to put me.'

'For your own good.'

'Rabbitch.'

If he goes on at me now, I thought, I may fall apart, give in to them all. I may cry. Dear God don't let me cry.

'I have told Bibi what is to happen about the child.'

'She is very perturbed about that you know. She's afraid this . . . chap may be most unsuitable. I mean to say, Constance, how do you know he's suitable? After all . . .'

'After all?'

'What do you know about him?'

'He's not beautiful.'

'I didn't ask you if he were. Suitable was the word I used. Suitable.'

'Suitable for what?'

'Will he cope with a child? Is he responsible ... caring ... responsible?'

'If he comes he will be all those things. If he doesn't come there's no problem. Bibi will do her best.'

'Wouldn't it be as well to leave it like that? Tidy?'

'Don't renege on me, Bill.'

'Let's have some more champagne.'

'Yes. There are two bottles to be drunk. Therapeutic. For you as well as me.'

He got up and collected the bottle from the table and poured some into each of our glasses. He looked a bit forlorn, a person no longer with any expectations. A shadow, like myself. I raised my glass towards him.

'The fools,' I said. 'Sad fools.'

'I won't renege. You know that.'

'Why don't you go, Bill, pack your stethoscope and go?'

'You really are a fool if you think it's as easy as that. Once you're on the gravy train there's no way off. It's not really up to me to decide any more. I can't cut off the goodies.' He clicked his finger. 'Just like that. They're so used to ... oh well, you know. They're so protected. I wouldn't have the heart to do that.'

'Heart?'

'Courage, if you prefer.'

'How do you know they won't all end up despising you? Hating you perhaps? Becoming Baader Meinhofs, because you could never see any alternative, because you destroyed them by giving them too much.'

'Don't be silly.'

'I'm not being silly. I'm not very bright, that's my major problem, but that's not the same thing as being silly. I was so certain that it was possible, essential really, yes, essential to see the whole thing through on my own. I found out though that all I was doing was protecting myself against pain. I wasn't beating a trail. I never fought. I became very adept at keeping my head down. Here I am, eyeball to eyeball with death, and I haven't moved the world in any way. I haven't even left a footprint on its surface. Next week, perhaps, it will be as if I had never existed. How sad, a few people will say and that will be that. Oh golly, I sound self-pitying . . . I'm not . . . I'm just trying to say the truth. We're not given much to work on, are we? A few pieces of jigsaw puzzle and too little time. I would just suggest that you stop taking the tonsils out of the rich and go and learn to live . . . learn to die really, because that's the only reality that there is. Before it is too late.'

'I don't take out tonsils. I get very well paid for suggesting that someone else should take them out.'

He laughed and then I laughed.

'How disgusting.'

'Yes, isn't it, quite disgusting. The trouble with champagne is that it evaporates so quickly. Snap, crackle and pop. An empty glass.'

'Pour us some more. Do you remember a lot of things, Bill? Tiny, happy things, like picnics at Brittas Bay and Calary Races?'

'Those things still happen.'

'Not Calary Races.'

'No, but you know what I mean. Those things still go on.'

'I think they must be very clear to me because I went away. The wind that always blew up on top of the mountain. I remember the feel of the five sixpences in my hand and the awful terror that I'd lose the bookie's ticket before the race was over. The sun was truly always shining, but the spring wind made it cold. I always had to keep searching for my ticket, feeling in all my pockets, in my gloves. You must remember how happy we were?'

'It all goes on. Brittas is overcrowded and we don't go to the races any more. The sun never seems to shine at all nowadays.'

'How long is it since you climbed the Sugar Loaf? I suppose your children do it instead. And Fossett's circus. Do you take your children to Fossett's circus? That was fantastic. We always came home with fleas, and had to have our heads examined for those other unmentionables. It was worth it though. Little flashes in and out of my mind, like movie stills. And those parties with flags on the sandwiches, banana, egg, tomato. No bananas during the war, the one great deprivation that I remember. And the conjuror . . . always the same poor man. I used to feel so sorry for him faced three times a week during the Christmas holidays with all those beastly scrubbed kids . . . always the few who didn't believe in magic, who knew how the tricks were done. Oh God, now I come to think of it you were one of them. One of the beasts. You always knew.'

He laughed.

'I always thought I knew, until I got home and tried it for myself. Someone gave me a box of tricks for Christmas once. A wand, some vanishing knots, a few bottomless cylinders . . . oh yes . . . a lot of coloured handkerchiefs. I was so dazzled by my own expertise I had dreams of becoming an illusionist . . . but then I took up fishing and I forgot. All the little bits and pieces got lost.'

'I might have married you, if you'd become an illusionist. You could have sawed me in half in all the capitals of Europe.'

'And America.'

'Of course. I could have worn black tights and spangles and looked after the bunnies.'

'What bunnies?'

'The ones that you pulled out of your top hat.'

'Ah no, ah no, Constance, you've got it all wrong. You are confusing the common or garden conjuror with the illusionist. I was intending to rise far, far above bunnies.'

'It would have been fun. Maybe we'd even have been happy.'

'It is extremely unlikely.'

'Yes, I suppose it is. It's nice to think though that there is a possibility of happiness. You have to believe in that possibility. Right to the end. Tomorrow I may be happy. How about you?'

'I doubt it.'

He picked up the bottle which was on the ground beside his chair and held it up to the light.

'Nearly dead.'

I laughed.

'To whom are you referring?'

'There's nothing so dead as a dead bottle.'

'There's another one in the fridge.'

'It's good. You don't often get good champagne these days.'

'My father was a man of discernment. I'm making a point of disposing of his drink before Bibi and Charles can lay their hands on it. Actually I can't drink wine, so you don't have to feel sorry for them. All that lovely claret will end up on their table.'

'God bless Barbara and Charles.'

He emptied his glass and stood up.

'I'll get the other bottle if I may and some food, if there's any about. I'm starving. How about you?'

I shook my head.

'I'm on a diet. You'll find all sorts of little dishes in the fridge. Delicious little dishes. Don't be too long.'

He looked at me from the doorway.

'Are you all right . . . ?'

'Oh yes. I just have a feeling that I'll never sit here again and drink champagne with you. Such an enjoyable pastime. Pass time. The bright day is done and we are for the dark . . . I . . . I am for the dark. Just don't be long.'

He went out and I was suddenly aware of Mother's presence in the room. She was standing by the window, her face expressionless. The firelight flickered over her pale skin.

'Mother.' I whispered the words, afraid that Bill might hear my voice. She didn't move. She was the most immobile ghost I had ever seen. Her eyes and her diamonds glittered, that was all. I dragged my eyes away from her and gazed into the living fire.

'You were right. There were all sorts of lovely things there. Look, I have a feast.'

He put the loaded tray on the table and began to open the second bottle.

'Ghosts come and go,' I said to him.

'Memories most probably. Pictures of the past. It must be hard to tell the difference.'

Pop.

'Ghosts, though, if that's what you want them to be. I wouldn't argue. Nothing unpleasant, I hope.'

He put a glass into my hand and began to pile a plate with food.

'Nothing unpleasant . . .'

She had gone. She didn't like the company of the living. I leaned back in my chair and closed my eyes. I couldn't bear to watch him eat. A thousand explosions of light patterned the darkness behind my eyelids. The blue lights from the tree and speaking diamonds, orange sparks from the fire, diamanté shoe buckles, the bobbing white lights of the fishermen and flickering candles. I could hear his voice talking on and on, but not the words that he was saying. My head ached with the lights. Nothing would stop their movement. Nothing.

'Constance, Constance.'

I forced my eyes to open. He was standing, so tall by the chair looking down at me.

'I'm all right,' I said. 'Quite all right.' I held my hand towards him and he took it. 'I just had my eyes closed. How terrible of me to close my eyes when you were talking to me.'

'I think you should go to bed. You look very, very tired. Probably feverish. You shouldn't be up. Come.'

'I'm all right. I promise you. Here, give me another drink. That'll perk me up.'

He shook his head.

'You've had enough.'

'Are you being mean?'

'Sensible.'

'I am tired. All of a sudden very tired. I feel as if I had climbed the Sugar Loaf. Imagine what it must be like up there . . . all the snow . . . perhaps I should go to bed. I don't want to, Bill. Will I just fade away . . . or will . . . will it be much worse than this? What will happen . . . ?'

He picked me up in his arms as if I were a child and turned me round so that I could see the tree. The flowering blue tree, reflected also in the dark window.

'Isn't it beautiful?'

'I asked you . . .'

'I don't know the answer. Look at the tree, dear Constance. Isn't it beautiful?'

'Yes.'

He carried me out of the room and across the hall. My room was warm and the bed turned back as it always used to be when we were children. I had a fever, he was right. Sweat was bursting out from under the rim of my hair and creeping down my face and neck. Uncomfortable.

He put me on the bed and began to unfasten my dress.

'I can do it. Let me . . . I can manage.'

He paid no attention to me. His hands were kind and cool. Wherever his fingers touched me more sweat burst out and spread over the battered surface of my body. He dried me with a towel and then wrapped me in my mother's old silk dressing-grown and pulled the bed clothes up over me.

'Pain?' he asked. 'Is it bad?'

I shook my head. He seemed huge. It was just an ache all over, a weary aching. I could live with it. He sat down on the bed beside me and took my hand.

* * *

Jacob Weinberg took her hand. She didn't look towards him. She felt the pressure of his mutilated thumb on her skin. She didn't look. Her eyes stared across the bay at the piazza, the tables and chairs outside the café, the bright umbrellas. The steps were golden and the cobbled street. This is what I will remember, she said in her mind. The brightness, the peace. The brown boys swimming; the tiny cathedral up on the rock above the town; sunlight splintering the blue sea. This I will tell the child. This picture I will hold in my mind until I can pass it on to the child.

'Permesso.'

A man with two straw baskets and a small girl wearing a straw hat pushed past her and went up the gangway.

'Constance, how inconstant you are.' He let go of her hand. 'You have forgotten me already.'

She turned and smiled at him.

'I was just trying to photograph that.' She nodded towards the square.

'Fix it in my mind . . . so that when I am bored or old or

157

glum . . . I can take the picture out and look at it.'

He shook his head.

'It never works out like that, Irish woman. You will remember strange things . . . things you have even now forgotten. They will turn out to be the moments of importance.'

He touched her cheek gently.

'We have been a little happy.'

She nodded. When she spoke her voice was very formal, almost cold.

'Thank you. You have been very kind to me.'

'Foolish.'

She held her hand out towards him. He touched it abruptly and then turned and walked away.

'Foolish, foolish person.'

She picked up her case and went up the gangway. The boat horn whooped a warning. People shoved themselves and their bundles towards the gangway. Ciao. The whole world was shouting the word. Ciao. A dog on the quay ran around in circles, barking at its tail. Arms waved, scarves, hats. The boys in the water waved. The men on the fishing boats. Ciao called the little girl in the straw hat to someone still on the land. Over the heads and the arms she could see him walking away, his shoulders hunched, his hands clenched in his pockets. Over the bridge that held the quayside to the land, through the cluster of parked cars and across the piazza, into the darkness of the climbing streets. He never looked back. At the pasticerria the street curved away from the harbour. He turned the corner. He never looked back. He was gone.

'I am not a fool.'

'Scusi?'

'Non è niente. Grazie.'

Grazie per tutto.

I am not a fool.

*　　*　　*

The bright day is done. There is someone moving across the room. I must open my eyes with care. Maybe it is someone I do not wish to see. Maybe my waiting mother is becoming impatient. She used to tap her foot on the carpet and call softly . . . Hurry, hurry, Constance, why is it always you . . . always . . . who are late? This time I'll surprise you, Mother dear. Twenty years early, give or take a year or two. My bright day is done. Fever makes me confused. Fact and fantasy stroll together in my head . . . and of course champagne.

'Don't wake her if she's asleep. I just popped in on the off chance.' Indubitably Bibi, her voice just loud enough to waken the almost dead.

'Have some champagne,' I said, keeping my eyes closed. 'There should be some left, unless Bill finished the bottle.'

'I thought you were asleep. I hope I didn't wake you. We were just passing on our way home from the Kennedys. I thought . . .'

'I can smell Mitsouko. Do have some . . . Bridie'll get the bottle and a glass. I'll open my eyes in a minute.'

I heard Bridie's feet cross the room.

'Don't bother, Bridie. I can only stay a moment. Charles is in the car.'

I opened my eyes. She was dressed in black as though I were already dead.

'You look like Mother. I've never noticed that before. Mother at her best.'

She touched her hair with a gloved hand and smiled faintly.

'Won't Charles come in? It must be freezing outside. Wouldn't he like a quick drink?'

'I just popped in to see that you were all right. I didn't like to pass the door. I won't stay. I gather Bill was here . . .'

'A cup of tea?' suggested Bridie.

'No, thank you.'

'Was it a good party?'

I wondered if there were flags on the sandwiches. A conjuror perhaps?

'So so. Too crammed, really. You know the way things are at this time of year. A bit circus-like. Angela said Bill was visiting patients.'

'So he was.'

'And drinking champagne?'

'Why not? Last call. Therapy. The doctor has to sit down and put his feet up some time.'

'I hope you're not going to cause any trouble.'

I started to laugh. I went on laughing for quite a while. The party spirit ebbed visibly away from Bibi's face. She smoothed her gloves and adjusted the belt of her fur coat.

'Why do you always have to make jokes out of things?'

'I'm sorry. Don't go, Bibi. Please don't go. Stay and talk to me. Tell me about the children. How are they? What are they up to? You're always in such a rush. Sit down. Coffee . . . Would coffee tempt you?'

'I must go. I promised Charles I'd only stay a minute. Tomorrow . . . we'll have a good old chat tomorrow.'

She waved a black hand. She blew me a kiss. She disappeared and with her the Mitsouko.

'She's not a bit like you,' said Bridie, after the hall door closed.

'You didn't know me in my heyday.'

She looked at me speculatively.

'I don't mean outside, inwardly she's not like you. She doesn't say funny things. I don't think she likes people much.'

'I don't think I do either.'

'You're all right.'

'You could fetch me the remains of the champagne and a glass for yourself.'

Off she went.

'The bright day is done . . .'

'What?' she called back from the hall.

'Just words. Words that keep running through my head. You know the way sometimes a little tune drives you mad, running in and out of your head for days. For no reason. These words are like that. They won't leave me alone.'

'What are they?'

She came in with the bottle. Bill hadn't done too badly after I had fallen asleep and there was just enough left for a glass each.

'Finish, good lady; the bright day is done and we are for the dark. Antony and Cleopatra, Shakespeare.'

'I've heard of Shakespeare.'

'A great man for words.'

'Those are sad words.'

'A bit.'

She sneezed.

'I sleep with my light on. I hope you don't mind. I've never liked the dark. All the lights were off at half ten and the curtains pulled tight. You couldn't see a thing, only hear the other girls breathing and the chairs creaking. On my own . . .'

She sneezed again.

'I don't think you'll ever make a serious champagne drinker.'

'Coke makes me sneeze too. Do you want your pills? You look all washed out.'

'I don't like the dark either . . . not total dark. I like to watch the pattern that the changing light makes on the ceiling. I like to know that the sun and moon are at their old routine. Yes, I'll have a couple of pills. Or did Bill give me some? I don't remember.'

'He didn't say. He just got up when I came in and put on his coat. Keep a good eye on her, he said. Nothing about pills. He looked tired. Then he went away.'

'I'll have a couple. After all they can't exactly do me any harm.'

The girl shook two pills out of the bottle and put them into the palm of my hand. I shoved them into my mouth and washed them down with the last drops in the glass. That should fix me for a few hours.

'Did you confess?' I asked the question merely so that she shouldn't go away, take herself off to her decorated bedroom where the light would burn all night.

'Yes.'

'I've always wondered if you feel different afterwards. Better? Or just unchanged, indifferent?'

Her navy blue dress had drab white spots on it and a cheap plastic belt.

'Lighter,' she said suddenly. Her fingers crumpled and then smoothed the drab cloth.

'Lighter,' I murmured.

'That's the word I'd use. That's the way I feel. Like when you've just had a bath and washed your hair. Quite, quite light.'

'I don't suppose you've much to confess really.'

'I used to hate people quite a lot . . . certain people . . . not everyone or anything like that. Just . . . certain people. Things like that. Disobedience, ingratitude, bad thoughts. I've even wanted to kill people. Wipe them off the face of . . .'

'We all do that at times. I don't think it's any great cause for worry. You have to set the bad thoughts off against the good ones . . . always remember, Birdie, that blind obedience can be more evil than wilful disobedience. It's all part of the process of learning. Each day we live we have so much to learn.'

'I wouldn't want to destroy my life with learning. I'd just like to be happy. Isn't that possible?'

'I'm sorry, I don't know.'

'Do you believe in God?'

'Sometimes.'

'How can you believe sometimes and not other times? That seems silly.'

'Yes. It does. It's the way it is though. I've never heard the whisper of His voice in any of the places we're told we should hear it. I listened and then after a time I gave up listening any more.'

My eyes began to fold themselves together. I could only dimly see her standing there by the bed, her fingers still moving on the surface of her dress. The light from my lamp cast chasm-like shadows on her young face. The animal inside me began its evening meal.

'Suddenly . . . I am so tired tonight . . . I have never heard the whisper . . . I haven't . . . but only because I haven't known how to listen. I have never found the silence in my heart that is necessary. Are you there?'

'I'm here.'

'I used to hate being young and yet I found no other time that was any better. What an epitaph. I mustn't keep you from your bed any longer. The bright day is done. Sleep well. Sleep.'

She pulled the covers up around me and smoothed at the sheets.

'Goodnight. If you want me, just call. I'll keep my door open. You sleep and don't let things be worrying you.'

*　　*　　*

The air hostess took the carry cot from Constance and carried it carefully down the steps. Great white clouds were heaped behind the hills. The sun was well on its way down. Constance hurried after the girl. She stumbled slightly at the foot of the steps.

'Ooops,' said the man behind her and put out a hand to steady her. 'Thanks.'

'We wouldn't want you to break a leg . . . not after safely landing . . . would we?'

The sun was reflected in the shallow puddles on the tarmac and in the windows of the airport buildings.

'Lucky to get a break between showers.' He was a chatty man.

'Yes. Very.'

'Awful bloody country for rain. Been here before?'

'Yes. I must . . .' She indicated the hostess with the baby and hurried on.

'I'll take her now. I can manage. Really I can.'

The girl smiled.

'I'll take her as far as the customs for you. Have you a lot of luggage?'

'No.'

'You'll be all right then. I'll get you a trolley when we get in to the building. She's been a very good passenger.'

'Yes.'

'It'll rain,' said the chatty man to someone behind her. 'You'll see. I'd give it half an hour. Never stops.'

Bibi was waiting outside the customs hall. Her face had no welcoming expression.

'There you are. The plane was on time for once. I was afraid I might be here all afternoon. Can I taken something? Is that all the luggage you have? I thought you'd be loaded down. I brought the big car.'

The sisters kissed and then Bibi looked casually into the cot. The baby slept untroubled. Her thick black lashes curled on to her cheek bone, one pale fist was raised in salute.

'Sweet,' said Bibi. She looked away quickly. 'The car's just over the road.'

They walked in silence across the crowded lounge and out into the car park. As Bibi unlocked the door of the car she looked once more at the child.

'Sweet,' she said again. 'She's very dark. Such a lot of lovely dark hair. Mine were all practically bald for ages. Ages.'

They manoeuvred the cot on to the back seat of the car. The baby opened her eyes and looked up at them. Shrewd black eyes stared for a moment at the two women and then closed into sleep again.

Bibi got in and opened the door for Constance. She fastened her seat belt and put the key in the ignition.

'She looks sort of Italian. Lovely . . . sweet . . . but Italian.'

'If you really want to know, her father is a Polish Jew.'

'Oh my God,' said Bibi.

The engine started. Four drops of rain burst on the windscreen.

'He was right.'

'Who?'

'The man who said it was going to rain.'

'Ttttt.'

'She's a very good baby.'

'I'm sure she is. She does look sweet. I didn't mean . . .'

'I know you didn't.'

'I mean, I don't mind what she is, you know that. Charles tends to be a teeny bit . . . well . . . anti-Semitic. Not anything bad, you know. He's old-fashioned. It's an old-fashioned prejudice . . . not that he'll . . .'

'Of course not.'

'And anyway, it's what you're brought up really isn't it, that counts.'

'I suppose so.'

'You haven't . . . Constance, you haven't taken any silly irrevocable steps, have you?'

'No. No steps at all. She hasn't even been baptised. I thought we'd wait and see . . .'

Bibi sighed and turned out on to the main road. The rain was coming down quite fiercely.

'I presume she has a name . . . at least.'

'Anna . . . at the moment. It's only a temporary name.'

'It sounds good enough to be a permanent one to me.'

Béal Feirste, pointed the sign post, Atha Cliath. Welcome home, child, I thought.

'Things have worked out very well. You remember old Josie?'

'I . .'

'Of course you do. She looked after the children when they were small. She's had this tiny flat in Ranelagh for years. She's been doing baby sitting and new babies, just making ends meet. She's a dear. The children see her regularly. She came to me last week in a terrible state because her landlord had put her rent up. Admittedly she'd been paying peanuts for years, but he put it up phenomenally. She hadn't a hope of managing. It was just after I got your letter. Now wasn't that amazing? I said to her, come back to us, Josie. My dear, she was overjoyed. She's back in her old room and just dying to get her hands on . . . umm, Anna. I think that's a lovely name. Jewish overtones, which after all . . .'

'Quite.'

'We've had the old nursery painted and I've dug out all sorts of things I thought we'd given away. You don't have to worry at all. Are you sure you won't spend tonight with us? We'd love to have you.'

'I want to get back to the house. Settled in.'

'Bill has arranged a bed for you in Vincents. Tomorrow you can go there. There didn't seem any point in wasting time.'

'I'm not going into hospital.'

'Constance, for heaven's sake, don't be silly. It's all arranged. It'll only be for a week or so. Assessment, I think they call it. So they can see what treatment you need. We have to get you fit again. A couple of weeks. Just till they find out what is . . .'

'I sent Bill a whole parcel full of papers telling me . . . telling anyone who wants to look at them what's wrong with me. I'm dying. And I'm bloody well going to die in peace without doctors and nurses being let loose on me with hatchets and tubes and needles and everyone else being cheerful and brave and pretending that I'm going to see a hundred. I've never wanted anyone to interfere with my life so leave me alone.'

'No need to shout.'

'You're great, Bibi. Great. Taking the baby. I don't know what I would have done if you hadn't been prepared to have her. I can never thank you enough for that.'

'You'd do as much for me.'

Constance doubted it.

'Is your stuff coming over by rail?'

She shook her head.

'What would I want all that rubbish for?'

'But . . .'

'The child's things are in the case. That's all I brought. A friend has taken over my flat and I told her to do what she liked with my things. Keep them, wear them, throw them out, give them to some charitable organisation. It's all the same to me. I've a few clothes with me. My toothbrush.'

'You are . . . just the same as ever.'

'Yes.'

'Look, are you sure you don't want to come home with me? There's a bed ready for you.'

'No. Drop me off at the house first. I'd rather it was like that. I don't want to . . . well, get messy over the baby or anything like that.'

They drove the rest of the way to Ballsbridge in silence.

The house looked the same as it had always looked, as if she had never been away. Behind the iron railings the grass was neat, the path trimmed. The door was painted dark green and the railings were glossy black. Constance fumbled in her bag for the key she had taken with her so long before. She held it up in front of Bibi's face.

'Look. How about that for efficiency?'

'I'll come in and show you where everything is.'

'It's okay. You needn't bother. I'll find my way around.'

'Father turned the dining room into a bedroom. He only used the one floor after . . . unless he had visitors. It seemed more sense. Will you be . . . ?'

'I'll be fine.'

'There's food in the fridge.'

'Thank you.'

'Well . . .'

'Goodbye.'

'I'll be round tomorrow. We'll have to talk seriously.'

'Yes.'

'Don't worry about Anna.'

'Who?'

'The . . .'

'Oh yes. No, I won't worry about her.'

'Goodbye.'

She pushed open the heavy gate. The hinges groaned slightly. They had always groaned slightly. Behind her she heard Bibi start the car and move slowly off along the road. There were still a few leaves on the trees. She held on to the railing as she climbed the high granite steps, as she had done as a very small child. Mind yourself, Constance, there's a good girl. Mind and don't fall. She opened the door and went into the hall. There was a smell of loneliness and dead flies.

She closed the door behind her. It was dark now in the hall. She sat down on the polished chair beside the door and all the unshed tears burst out of her eyes and through her shielding fingers on to her knees, like the rain outside which was beating in little gusts against the windows.

* * *

Mother smiled as I drowned. She sat in a green velvet chair by the edge of the sea. Over her head seagulls circled and mewed like angry cats. I knew that when my body would finally float to the surface they would be waiting for me; waiting to sink their beaks into my dead, salt-soaked flesh. Coils of mermaids' hair twisting round my legs pulled me deeper into the boiling sea. She smiled and raised her hand in some kind of benediction. Hot salty water washed over my head and ran down my face. The salt stung my eyes, clung to the corners of my mouth. Finish good lady, Shakespeare himself calling from under the water, the bright day is done, a sonorous voice, my head was filled with sound of it, and we are for the dark. Mother, I called. She smiled. Mother, the bright day is done. More weed grasped at my arms. Mother.

Bridie was leaning over me. The cool cloth in her hand wiped the sweat from my face.

'There,' she whispered. 'There. You'll be all right now.'

Mother's dressing-gown, the sheets, the pillow cases were drenched and cold, I was shivering. The sea couldn't have been boiling, I thought. Bridie was in her dressing-gown, her face crumpled by sleep.

'A nightmare. Just . . . I'll be all right.'

'Let me help you out of there and I'll change your sheets.'

'I . . .'

'You'll do as I say.'

She lifted me out of the bed and carried me across the room. She put me gently down in the armchair.

'You're drowned. It's like as if you'd been in a bath.'

She took off the silk dressing-gown and wrapped me in a towelling one from the back of the door. Then she tucked a blanket over me and began to strip the bed.

'I'm sorry. I'm sorry to have woken you.'

'Isn't that what I'm here for? Don't give a thought to it.'

She folded each sheet neatly and laid them over the back of a chair and then did the same with the pillow cases.

'Isn't it lucky I did all that washing yesterday? There's lots of clean sheets in the hot press. I'll just get them. I'll put the kettle on. I'm sure you could do with a cup of tea.'

'I called for my mother.'

'Yelled,' she said. 'That was what woke me up. The yells of you.'

She picked up the sheets and left the room.

I must have dropped off asleep, because when I opened my eyes next she was just tucking in the last corner neatly, as she had been taught to do in the home.

'It's a funny thing.'

She turned and smiled at me as I spoke.

'I never called for my mother when she was alive. She was never very sympathetic towards . . . isn't that odd? She would have been the last person.'

'Sometimes I do the same thing myself . . . now isn't that odder?'

We both laughed. It hurt me to laugh. I will have to confine myself to smiling in future.

'I'll help you into bed and then you can have a nice cup of tea.'

'I don't think I can move.'

'It's lucky I'm a big strong girl.'

She picked me up.

'A feather,' she said. 'I could run a mile with you.'

The bed embraced my bones. Gently she pulled the covers up around me.

'What time is it?'

'About half four. It's Christmas Eve.'

'Christmas Eve? So it is. Turn on the tree, Bridie. If you leave my door open and the door across the hall, maybe I will be able to see it from here.'

'I'll do that. But take your sup of tea first.'

She held the cup to my mouth. I took a sip, just to please her and then shook my head.

'That's enough.'

'A little sup more.'

'I can't.'

'Some water then? I'm sure you should drink something.'

'No. Not at the moment. In the morning. I promise you I will do me best then. Porridge, bacon and eggs and fried bread. Lovely fried bread. That's something I haven't had for years . . . with marmalade on it.'

She laughed.

'You cod, you.'

She went over to the door and switched off the light.

'I hope you get some sleep.'

'I'll sleep.'

She crossed the hall and went into the study.

'Can you see that?'

A blue pyramid of light floated in the darkness.

'Yes.'

'It's lovely.'

'Yes. Go to bed, Bridie. Sleep too. Say a prayer for me. A kind prayer.'

'Yes, I'll do that.'

'Goodnight so.'

The lovely blue lights hypnotised me into sleep.

*　*　*

These last few pages are written by me Bridie May, beginning on Christmas Eve 1978. I haven't made anything up, nor have I left anything out . . . at least I don't think I have. Before I left Dublin, two days after Christmas, I wrapped up all her papers and put them into the post addressed to Dr Bill Hurley, 6 Cross Avenue, Blackrock. I registered the parcel as she told me to. I hope it got to its destination.

*　*　*

After all that business in the middle of the night I didn't wake till all hours . . . or what would have been considered all hours in the Home. It was half nine. I hopped out of bed like a scalded cat and got dressed. I went in to see if she was all right. She was lying as I had left her the night before, only all those papers of hers were scattered on the bed and floor. Her eyes were open and she was watching the snowflakes falling down past the window, piling up on the ledge, making a little wall.

'Don't turn on the light,' says she. 'It's nice like this, the snow falling on one side of me and the tree over there on the other. Veritable Christmas.' I remember the word, because she repeated it several times. Veritable.

'How about the bacon and eggs and fried bread?' says I to her.

She smiled a little.

'I think not. Get me a glass of water, would you, a tincture of whiskey to make it palatable and some pills. What could be better than that.'

I knew she must be feeling pretty rough because she didn't like to take the pills unless she was in a poor way. I got the water from the kitchen and mixed in some whiskey. I had to put my arm under her to help her sit up so that she could drink. All power seemed to have left her limbs. I took two pills from the bottle and held them out to her.

'Let's be dogs and have four,' says she.

I wondered if Dr Bill would mind, but I couldn't see that he would, so I gave her the extra two. It was after that she asked me to write everything down.

'Everything . . . but, Bridie, no flights of fancy. Just straight, put it down straight. No flights.'

She watched me without saying a word while I gathered up her papers and tidied the room a bit. There were some notebooks and some loose typewritten pages and a couple of blue files.

'Take them. Put them in your room or somewhere. Mind them.'

'I'll mind them.'

She nodded.

I took the papers and put them in my room and then got on with my work. I wanted the place to be clean for Christmas. Shining for God, one of the sisters used to say. She wasn't one of the ones I liked. I popped my head round the door several times. She didn't move. I wondered if I should ring Dr Bill, but just as I was putting on the kettle for a cup of tea about eleven the bell rang and he was standing there, covered with snow on the door mat. He shook himself like a dog before he came into the hall. His shoes left muddy marks on my nice polished floor.

'How is she?' he asked.

I told him about the trouble in the night. I whispered it to him. I didn't want her to hear us saying things about her, in case she would be worried. He chewed at his lower lip and nodded his head as I spoke. I asked him if he'd stay a few minutes while I ran round to the launderette with the dirty bedclothes. I hated the thought of them lying there over Christmas, and anyway we might be needing them. He nodded again and went into her room and closed the door.

I forgot to turn down the kettle and by the time I got back it was hopping on the gas like a step dancer, but luckily there was still a few drops of water in the bottom, so no harm was done. I could hear his voice coming from the other room, but not the words he was saying. I could hear nothing from her at all. He came out at last and into the kitchen.

'I'll tell you what we'll do, Bridie,' says he. 'We'll carry the damn tree into her room. I think that'd make her happy.'

We unplugged the lights and carried the tree into her room. We put it on a little table in the corner opposite her bed, where she could see it without any trouble. At first the lights wouldn't work when he plugged them in, but we twisted at the bulbs for a few minutes and then all was well.

'A loose connection,' says he.

She smiled and whispered something that I didn't catch. Her teeth suddenly looked far too big for her face, as if they should have belonged to someone else. Maybe this is a flight of fancy.

'I'll be back later, Constance. You'll be all right till then.'

He came out into the hall where I was waiting.

'I'm sorry about this, Bridie.' I helped him on with his coat. 'It's not a very nice way to spend Christmas.'

'There'll be other Christmases,' says I. What else was there to say?

'I don't think she'll bother you. Just see that she's comfortable. If she'll take the odd drink, so much the better. Pills. Perhaps she might need pills. I'll be back. If Mrs Barry comes round just say that she's asleep, there's a good girl. Don't say anything else unless I tell you to. Asleep. Not to be disturbed.'

He walked slowly towards the door and stood by it for a moment before opening it. I wondered if there had ever been anything between them. Anything romantic. But she wouldn't like me to be writing that.

'Bridie,' says he at last. 'Are you frightened?'

'No.' I told him a lie.

'Good girl.'

He opened the door and the snow swirled in as he went out.

I looked in at her. She was peaceful, just looking at the tree. I went and got out the dustpan and brush and cleared up the mess of dust and tiny needles we'd made as we moved the tree.

Everything was now shining for Christmas.

Mrs Barry didn't come round, but she phoned just after I had my lunch.

'How is Miss Constance?'

'She's asleep.'

'I've been up to my eyes today as you can imagine, but I'll try and get round later on today. Are you managing all right?'

'Fine. The doctor's been.'

'What did he say?'

'He said to let her sleep. Sleep is very good for her, he said. Just let her sleep, Bridie. She needs to . . .'

'Do you need anything in the house? Is there any shopping or anything I can do?'

'No. There's so much food in the fridge it'll take about a week to get through it.'

'Good. As I said, I'll try to get round later. We have people coming this evening so I may not manage . . . but you will ring me if you have any worries? Any worries at all? You will, won't you?'

I will in my eye.

'Yes, Mrs Barry,' says I.

I went and sat in with her and did the writing she had told me to do. She slept for a while, her breath panting out of her like someone who has run a very long way. When she woke, she whispered my name. I went over to the bed.

'Is it Christmas yet?'

'Not yet.'

'It's taking such a long time, isn't it?'

'Would you like a drink?'

'Nothing.'

She looked at the tree for a long time.

'Dying is such a tiring business.'

She closed her eyes. For a moment I thought she had gone and my heart started to thump inside me like a hammer, but then I realised the breath was still puffing in and out of her, so I went and sat down and got on with my writing.

One of the nuns had died and we were made to go and look at her. She was very small and very old, really shrunk with old age. I shut my eyes as I walked up to the bed so I never knew what she looked like lying there dead. Some of the girls said she looked lovely. I didn't believe them as she had never looked lovely when she was alive.

Dr Bill came again as he had said. She was asleep and he sat on the bed by her and held her wrist in his fingers. Her hand looked enormous on the end of her starved arm.

'Listen.' He laid her hand down on the bed cover again. 'Is there a bed for me to . . . ? No, there's the sofa in the study. That will do me fine. Can you find me some bedclothes?'

'Yes, surely.'

'That's a girl. I'll go on home and have a bite of food and clear it with my wife. I'll stay here until you've been to church tomorrow morning. Then I'll have to go. Christmas and all that . . . Home . . . you know. Will that be . . . ?'

'Of course.'

He went away then and came back about two hours later. He sat in the room with her for a long time and then I heard him cross the hall and go to bed.

It was an odd sort of a Christmas day. I got up early and looked in at her. She was asleep, shrinking away into the pillows as you looked at her. The doctor snored in the other room. I pitied his wife having to put up with a racket like that night in, night out.

The snow had stopped and the sun was shining. Everything looked perfect, shining for God, clean and happy. The church was packed.

He was up and had made breakfast by the time I got back.

'Bacon and eggs, Bridie,' he called when he heard me coming in. 'You're just in time.'

He wasn't a bad cook at all, for a man.

'How is she?'

'Very weak. Maybe she'll last until tomorrow, maybe not. Don't say a word to anyone though.'

'No.'

'We wouldn't want to spoil their Christmas.'

'No.'

After he had gone I went to look through the records, thinking that a bit of music might be a good idea, but there wasn't anything there that I had ever heard of before, so I didn't bother.

Mrs Barry rang.

'Happy Christmas, Bridie.'

'Happy Christmas, Mrs Barry.'

'How's the invalid today?'

'She's asleep at the moment.'

'Did she have a good night?'

'Yes.'

'I'm sorry I didn't get round, but I knew you'd have let me know if anything . . .'

'Yes.'

'Tomorrow ... once Christmas is ... I'll be round tomorrow without fail. I'll bring all our presents round and the children are dying to see ...'

'Yes.'

'You'll tell her when she wakes.'

'Yes. I'll tell her.'

'And if there's anything ... You'll be sure ... won't you?'

'Yes.'

I put down the receiver.

The day just went on. The house was very quiet. I wondered how long the bulbs on the tree would last if we kept them on night and day. I wasn't lonely. I have to say I was a little uneasy, but not lonely. I did feel free like I had never done before. I wondered what was going on in her head. I hoped no more nightmares. Was she already dead in her head though not in her body? Flight of fancy?

I was on my way to bed when Dr Bill arrived again. He looked very pale and the smell of drink from him was quite strong.

'A happy Christmas to you, Bridie,' he said as he came in the door. He handed me a parcel with fancy ribbons on it. Gold and silver ribbons tied in great big bows. I looked at it for ages, or it must have been for ages because he said, 'Aren't you going to open it?' I looked up at him. He had taken off his coat and flung it all wet across the back of a chair. I picked at the bows, not wanting to spoil the ribbon. He put down some more parcels on the table.

'Is she ... ?'

'Still asleep.'

I unwrapped the white tissue paper and found a beautiful silk scarf, patterned all over with gold and yellow flowers, like something a film star would wear.

'I hope it's okay. My wife says I'm hopeless at buying presents.'

He was edging towards the door, not quite wanting to leave me to open the parcel on my own.

'It's gorgeous. That's two presents I got.' I held out my hand to show him the ring. 'Beautiful presents.'

'Perhaps next year you'll get twenty-two.'

'Get on with you.'

He nodded towards the boxes on the table.

'I've brought some turkey and mince pies and things. A lump of plum pudding and some brandy. Give me a call when you have everything set out and I'll come and join you for a picnic.'

I ate the food he had brought and he picked at a little to keep me company and drank quite a lot of brandy. He didn't speak much and I didn't like to disturb his thoughts. He poured some brandy over the plum pudding and then turned out the kitchen light. He lit a match and held it to the plate and a lovely blue flame danced in the darkness. I had never seen that done before. We both ate the pudding in silence and then he got up and held out his hand to me.

'I have to go home now. My wife . . . she expects me home. You understand. I don't think anything will happen. I'm sorry I have to go.'

I shook his hand.

'Goodnight, doctor, and thank you.'

'It is you we all have to thank.'

I suppose I shouldn't write that down.

He went into the room and spent about ten minutes in there. He didn't speak after. He just walked across the hall and out the door. I could hear his feet scrunching on the snow as he went down the steps. I was tired and left the washing-up until the morning. That's freedom for you.

*   *   *

In the morning she was white like a ghost, as if all the blood had drained out of her in the night. I covered her hands, which still lay outside the bedclothes with a little pink rug that she had used sometimes to wrap around her shoulders to keep the draughts away. I could just see the movement of her breathing. The Christmas tree was still alight. I passed my time by scrubbing the kitchen floor and clearing out the cupboards. They hadn't been touched for months by the look of them. There were even mouse droppings at the back of one. Luckily, I didn't meet a mouse.

Some time after eleven the bell rang. I wiped my hands dry and went to the door expecting to find Mrs Barry there. A funny looking little man in a big black hat was standing there, holding in his arms a baby.

'Yes?'

'Is this the house of Constance Keating?'

He spoke funny. He must have been foreign, not English, really foreign.

'Yes, but . . .'

He stepped past me into the hall. There was no stopping him. He handed the baby to me. I didn't mind. I've always been good with babies. It was hard to tell if it was a boy or a girl, but it smiled at me. No teeth. He took off his hat and shook snowflakes onto the floor. Then he put it on the chair by the door.

'She is expecting me.'

'I don't . . .'

'Jacob Weinberg is my name. She is expecting me. I have come as soon as I have got her letter. Who are you?'

'I'm Bridie May. I'm helping . . . looking after . . . she's not well you know.'

'I know. Where is she? I must . . .'

I nodded towards the door of her room. I wondered what the doctor would say.

'She's asleep at the moment.'

'That is my child,' says he, in a warning sort of voice. 'Her name is from today Zelda. I call her for my mother. You mind her well.'

I nodded. Nobody had told me that this was going to happen. I hoped no one would be cross with me. He turned and walked over to the door. He opened it very quietly and went into the room. He closed the door behind him. I waited a moment in the hall and then went into the kitchen and sat with the baby on my knee waiting to see what would happen. I could hear his voice blathering away in the other room. Talking to himself. It didn't sound like English he was speaking. Blather. The baby made baby noises at me and smiled again. Still no teeth. After about fifteen minutes I tiptoed across the hall and opened the door. Maybe he was doing something dreadful to her. He was standing by the bed with his arms stretched out, blathering away. Millions of names it sounded like to me foreign names, but then maybe it wasn't. His hands looked as if someone had taken a hammer to them.

'It is all right now, Bridie May. You can come in. She is dead.'

He said it quite calmly, as if death was no surprise to him.

'Oh Mother of God.'

I nearly dropped the baby in my fright when he spoke the word. I shut my eyes so that I wouldn't see her and then opened them again. He came over and took the baby from me and stood with her in his arms looking down at the bed.

'See. Come see.' He ordered me. 'It is only death. Come.'

I crept over and stood beside him. She didn't look one bit changed.

'She was alive half an hour ago,' I said. It was a silly thing to say. That's what death is. Here one minute, gone the next. I tried to pull myself together. I knew there were prayers that I should say. I blessed myself. That was right. But then my mind had nothing in it, only her own words that she had said.

'Finish, good lady; the bright day is done and we are for the dark.'

He looked at me and smiled. I blushed.

'I should have said, may she rest in peace.'

'She will.'

He held the baby out towards her.

'Zelda,' he said.

We stood in silence.

'I will go now. There is no point to stay. You will also come?'

I didn't know what he meant.

'You will come? I will need someone to mind Zelda for me. Someone to mind her well.'

'I . . .'

But after all why not, I thought. Why not?

'Away? Away from here?'

'Away.'

'I couldn't leave her alone,' I said. 'Perhaps I could come later.'

'Yes.'

He walked towards the door. I wondered should I cover her face.

'The Hibernian Hotel. Do you know . . .'

'Yes.'

'I will wait there for you until this evening. Then I go. I have had little trabble with the aunt about the baby. But I win. I do not want to stay for more trabble. If you do not want to come you must telephone me. I will wait there until this evening.'

He put on his hat and opened the door. I saw that a taxi was waiting outside the gate. He smiled at me.

'Jacob Weinberg. You will see, now everything will be all right.'

The steps were slippery with frozen snow, but he managed. He held the baby tight against him to keep her warm. At the gate he turned and bowed to me. I watched until the taxi had turned the corner and then went to ring Dr Bill.

There is no more to write. The house is full of people. The first thing Mrs Barry did when she arrived was turn off the lights on the tree and pull the curtains. How sad, I thought. How lonely to be dead and in the dark.

I have packed my case and I am sitting in my room writing this last page. When I have finished it I will put it in the parcel with the other papers and wrap them up with string and sellotape and go to the Hibernian Hotel.

February 1981

ANDREA LEVY

Never Far From Nowhere

By the author of *Every Light In The House Burnin'*,
Andrea Levy's new novel tells the story of two sisters,
Olive and Vivien, born in London to Jamaican parents
and brought up on a council estate. They go to the
same grammar school but whereas Vivien's life
becomes a chaotic mix of friendships, youth clubs,
skinhead violence, A-levels, discos and college, Olive,
three years older and a skin shade darker, has a very
different tale to tell . . .

'Andrea Levy is the long-awaited birdsong of one
born black and gifted in Britain. Let her sing and sing
and sing' Marsha Hunt

'Painfully perceptive and passionate, *Never Far From
Nowhere* hits a raw nerve with its powerful concoction
of poignancy and humour' *Pride*

'In this lively, crisp, raw voice, young black
Londoners may have found their Roddy Doyle'
Independent on Sunday

'Passionate and angry' *TLS*

0 7472 5213 0

review

ISLA DEWAR

Giving Up on Ordinary

When Megs became a cleaner, she didn't realise that if people looked at her a cleaner would be all they saw. Megs has as full a life as the people she does for, Mrs Terribly Clean Pearson or Mrs Oh-Just-Keep-It-Above-The Dysentery-Line McGhee. She's the mother of three children and still mourning the death of a son; she enjoys a constant sparring match with her mother; she drinks away her troubles with Lorraine, her friend since Primary One; and she sings the blues in a local club.

Megs has been getting by. But somehow that's not enough any more. It's time Megs gave up on being ordinary . . .

'Explosively funny and chokingly poignant . . . extraordinary' *Scotland on Sunday*

'Observant and needle sharp . . . entertainment with energy and attack' *The Times*

'A remarkably uplifting novel, sharp and funny' *Edinburgh Evening News*

0 7472 5550 4

review